Blood Will Have Blood

The peaceful town of Silver Spur is horrified when the Holby family is murdered, and suspicion immediately falls upon a stranger who had recently been in town asking for directions to the Holby farm. Sheriff Jack Kincade tracks the man to a neighbouring town, where he finds the stranger who introduces himself as Snake Holby, the murdered man's brother.

Jack takes Snake back to Silver Spur and locks him in jail for his own safety, as the townsfolk are convinced of his guilt, even though Snake claims that he didn't go to his brother's farm after all, being too ashamed of his shady past. Then a local boy tells the Sheriff how he had overheard three men talking about how they had massacred the family as an act of revenge.

So who did kill the Holby family? Jack and Snake set out to discover the culprits, but the trail is not so straightforward....

Blood Will Have Blood

Lee Lejeune

A Black Horse Western
ROBERT HALE

© Lee Lejeune 2016
First published in Great Britain 2016

ISBN 978-0-7198-1997-1

The Crowood Press
The Stable Block
Crowood Lane
Ramsbury
Marlborough
Wiltshire SN8 2HR

www.crowood.com

Robert Hale is an imprint
of The Crowood Press

The right of Lee Lejeune to be identified as
author of this work has been asserted by him
in accordance with the Copyright, Designs
and Patents Act 1988

Typeset by Catherine Williams, Knebworth

Printed and bound in Great Britain by
CPI Group (UK) Ltd, Croydon CR0 4YY

CHAPTER ONE

It was around noon when the stranger came into the Long Branch Saloon and perched himself on a high stool at the bar. The Long Branch's owner, Kev Stanley, noticed that he was tall and lean and had a hungry look about him. His range clothes were dusty and well-worn, suggesting he had spent many days in the saddle. He wore a gun belt with an old Navy Cap and Ball thrust into a well-worn holster. Judging by his looks, he was a drifter who travelled from one location to another without settling down anywhere.

'What can I get for you, mister?' Kev Stanley asked genially. He liked to be sociable even when he didn't care for the look of a man.

The stranger pushed back his battered Stetson to reveal a face that was tanned and lined like old rawhide, though he couldn't have been more than thirty-five or forty years old.

'You can get me a beer,' he said in a voice like a growling bear with a sore head.

Kev Stanley pulled a pint of beer and held it towards the stranger across the bar. The stranger seized the glass and took a long swig and placed the glass on the bar. Kev named the price and the stranger fished in his vest pocket and found his money and handed it across the bar. That's when Kev noticed the scar on his right cheek, running right down from below his eye to just above his chin. Probably caused by a bowie knife or even a bear's claw. It gave the stranger a curious look as though he was about to sneer but couldn't quite get there.

'You ridden far?' Kev asked him.

The stranger took another long swig of his beer and placed his empty glass on the bar. 'Give me the same again,' he ordered in the same growling tone.

Kev pulled another pint and placed the glass on the bar. As the stranger raised the glass, Kev saw that he was wearing an unusual ring on his right hand like a curved serpent biting its own tail. This time the stranger drank more slowly. He looked across the bar and seemed to focus on Kev for the first time. 'You know this country?' he said in a neutral tone.

Kev nodded and grinned. 'Lived here most all my life. So I reckon I know it pretty well.'

The stranger closed one eye for a moment. 'Then you can point me in the direction of the Matt Holby spread.'

'Matt Holby!' Kev exclaimed. 'Everyone around here knows Matt Holby and his good wife Mary. They live just a piece up the road from here, no more than a mile or two. You ride up the trail here ...' Kev pointed off to the right. 'You can't miss it. Big white sign with steer horns on the gate from the time it was a ranch.'

'Well, I'm obliged for that,' the stranger said in the same neutral tone. He got down from the bar stool and walked over to the swing doors. Kev saw that his legs were slightly bowed, no doubt from all those days in the saddle.

After the swing doors had flapped to, Kev came from behind the bar and peered out for a closer look at the

6

stranger. The man's horse was drinking at the trough. It was a big, strong piebald horse and looked in excellent condition in contrast to its master who was kind of flea-bitten.

'That's a damned fine beast,' Kev said to himself. 'From the look of the hombre, I would guess he stole it some place.' He took a mental note of the fact in case it might come in useful later.

Kev was the sort of man who prided himself on noticing details. He had seen a lot in his time: barroom brawls, fist fights, and the occasional shooting. Once he had had to bring his shotgun up from behind the bar to protect himself from a well-known gunman who was so drunk he could hardly hold a gun let alone aim and fire it.

Kev watched the stranger mount up and ride off in the direction of the Holby spread. The clock behind the bar suddenly struck the half hour. It was only thirty minutes since the stranger had ridden in.

'Didn't hang about long, did he?' came a throaty voice from the corner.

'Said he was looking for the Holby place,' Kev replied.

The man at the table got up and ambled over to the bar. He was Tiny Broadhurst, which was a contradiction in terms since he must have weighed in at 220 pounds at least. Tiny claimed to have accomplished great deeds in the recent war and he prided himself on his knowledge of men and his courage in the face of the enemy. Nobody knew how many medals he had gained or which battles he had fought in, but he reckoned he had done his duty for the cause and had earned the respect of the community. To celebrate his prowess, he spent most of his time drinking in the Long Branch Saloon.

'What d'you think?' Tiny croaked.

'What do I think about what?' Kev responded. Sometimes he found it difficult to be patient with his most persistent customer. Tiny Broadhurst was like a troublesome fly you had to flap away from your dinner but you can't just flap away a man as big as Tiny Broadhurst.

'What d'you think about that stranger?' Tiny asked him.

'What am I supposed to think?' Kev replied. He turned to look at the man looming over the bar. 'What do you think about him yourself?'

'Seems mighty suspicious to me,' Tiny replied. 'What does he want with the Holbys, anyway? Folks like that won't want to be seen dead with a saddle bum like that. Stands to reason, don't it?'

Kev poured himself a whiskey. 'You going home to eat?' he enquired.

Tiny raised a suspicious eyebrow. 'I might stick around and have something here,' he said, 'or I might step over to Bridget's place and take something there. Bridget does a real good meat pie, you know.'

'Well, that's fine.' Kev said, 'cause there's nothing for you here. The chef's taken sick.'

'You mean Alfredo's gone sick?'

'That's what I said, didn't I?' Kev replied none too pleasantly.

Tiny gave a high-pitched snigger. 'Hope it ain't food poisoning, Kev.'

'No,' Kev said. 'Just can't get up from the pan. As soon as he does, he has to rush back again in case he craps his pants.'

Tiny's mouth fell open. 'Then maybe I should go over to Bridget's place after all.'

'I think maybe you should.'

*

After the big man had steered himself across Main Street to Bridget's diner, Kev smiled to himself. It was peaceful in the Long Branch Saloon except for a solitary fly trying to commit suicide against a window pane. It wasn't that Kev disliked Tiny Broadhurst; it was that he found him damned irritating most of the time. After all, he didn't have the greatest brain in the world and what he called conversation was somewhat limited in range from 'how I won the war' to 'how I wrestled with that pesky bear'. Listening to how a man had wrestled with a bear got a little tiresome after you'd heard it seventeen times!

Kev's mind turned to the saddle tramp and his two pints of beer. Must have been awful thirsty to drink that much fluid in such a short time. Like he hadn't taken in anything for a month or more. And what can the man have wanted at the Holby place, anyway? Matt Holby wasn't into hiring hands. He had to do everything himself, though his wife Mary did a good deal to help, too. The Holbys were good folk who deserved to make their way in the world.

As he was thinking on the stranger and the Holbys, a door opened at the back of the saloon and a woman looked out.

'You ready to eat, Kev?' she called.

'I sure am,' Kev said. 'There's nobody in at the moment. That pestilential Tiny Broadhurst has just gone over the main drag to eat some of Bridget's meat pie.'

'Well then, put up the closed sign and we can eat here in the back.'

When it came to food, Kev always deferred to his wife Sophia. She was an excellent cook but she rarely cooked for the customers of the Long Branch. That was down to the unfortunate Alfredo who at that moment was at home squatting on the pan.

Bridget Kincade was behind the counter of what she called her Happy Eater, which was officially Bridget's Diner, when the somewhat substantial form of Tiny Broadhurst loomed in the doorway.

'You got some of that meat pie for me today, Bridget?' he shouted in his shrill croaky voice across the diner.

The place was pretty well full but nobody stopped eating to look up; they were all used to the big man's high-pitched croak.

'Come on in, Tiny!' Bridget greeted. 'I think I can spare you a little of the pie. How come you're not eating over at Kev's place?'

'Alfredo's off sick,' Tiny said. 'Got some kind of gut infection. Kev said he can't get up from the pan in case he …'

'Yeah, we heard about that,' someone said. 'Right now we're eating our chow and we don't want to hear about all that sitting on the pan stuff.'

'Sorry, Sheriff,' Tiny said in a more subdued tone. He walked between the tables and stood in front of Jack Kincade, the sheriff. 'Mind if I join you at the trough, Sheriff?'

Jack Kincade looked up and waved his knife. 'Be my guest, but don't talk about crapping or bears and we'll get along just fine.'

Tiny sat down at the sheriff's table and raised his knife and fork, ready to stab into his pie. He was usually too idle to walk over from the Long Branch and Bridget's diner was a real treat, specially on pie day!

Jack Kincade went on eating and his wife Bridget

scooped up another portion of the pie and brought it to the table. Running the diner and being sheriff of the town worked well for the couple. The town of Silver Spur was usually quite peaceable, even sleepy, and Jack Kincade's meal often stretched right on into early evening when the two children came home from school. Nobody seemed to care just as long as he wore his badge of office and was ready to deal with the rabble rousers and cowpokes who occasionally hit town.

Tiny stabbed the pie with his knife and fork and stuffed a large slice into his mouth. He wanted to say something but bears and crapping were off limits so he didn't know how to begin.

'Hey, Sheriff,' he said, with particles of pie spilling from his mouth, 'did you see that saddle bum hit town just before midday?'

'Can't say I did,' the sheriff murmured, trying not to look at the chunks of meat and pie on Tiny's shirt front.

'Didn't give his name,' Tiny added. 'Downed two pints of beer in two minutes flat.'

'Is that a record?' Jack Kincade asked with a grin.

'Well, he didn't have no pot belly or nothing, so I reckon he must have been awful thirsty. Like a rat just crawled in from the hot desert. Asked the way to the Holbys' place, too.'

'Did he now?' Jack Kincade looked at him with a little more interest.

'Sure he did. And Kev pointed right off and gave him directions. Couldn't have been in the Long Branch more than half an hour. I know because the clock behind the bar chimed the half hour just after he left. You know the clock I mean?'

The sheriff knew the clock well enough. It was Kev

Stanley's pride and joy. 'So didn't the stranger say who he was or what he wanted?'

'He didn't say much at all,' Tiny said. 'He was a real closed mouth hombre. Just ordered two beers and asked for directions which Kev gave him. He was a real flea-bitten hombre but he was riding a real nice piebald horse. That horse was in prime condition and I guess he might have stolen it from some place close by.'

'I saw that hoss,' a man from the next table said. 'Just before I came in for my pie. And Tiny's right; I think that down-at-heel saddle bum must have stolen it from some place.'

'Well, you might be right at that,' Jack Kincade said. He whipped his mouth clean and went to the door of the diner and looked in the direction of the Holbys' place which was no more than two miles away, close to the trail.

Next morning, Jack Kincade and his wife Bridget were sitting in Bridget's Diner having breakfast. The two children had gone off to school. The diner was officially closed and Jack liked to start the day with a good hearty breakfast. Breakfast was by his reckoning the most important meal of the day. Sometimes he didn't eat anything for the rest of the day, except on meat pie day, of course!

'Jack,' his wife had advised recently, 'I think you're being a little too generous with your victuals. You're beginning to get a little … I don't like to say it … stout in the midriff.'

Jack looked mildly amused. 'Fat!' he said with a smile, patting his paunch. 'That's not fat. There's hard muscle under there.'

Bridget smiled back politely. 'Well, if that's muscle there's a hell of a lot of it.'

Jack wasn't offended. Bridget and he had that kind of relationship; they could kid one another without taking offence. Bridget was still a handsome woman who wore good clothes and though Jack was a little out of condition, he had once been a handsome and well-groomed man. They had met in the East and it had been love at first sight. They had two children, a boy and a girl. The girl, Stephanie, was rising twelve and she helped in the diner sometimes. The boy, Gregory, was two years younger and he was as sharp as a tack. Bridget and Jack wanted him to go to law school some place, but that was expensive.

Jack got up from the table and dabbed his mouth again. 'I think I'll push off to the creek and do a little fishing. If I'm lucky we could have fish pie tomorrow. How would that be?'

'That would be just fine,' his wife said. 'Just as long as you don't doze off and fall in the river.'

Jack took his hat and was about to put it on when something happened that sent the fishing trip right out of his mind. There came a sudden thumping on the door of the diner.

'Sheriff Kincade!' a man shouted from outside.

Jack opened the door to reveal a man with a face as yellow as curled up parchment.

'What's the problem, Jerry?' the sheriff asked the man.

'Something awful's happened!` the man gasped.

'Well, you'd better step right inside and tell me about it,' Jack invited. His advice to himself since he had been made sheriff was never to panic. A man who panicked made bad decisions and that could lead to bad consequences.

Jerry was a farmer who had a spread further along the trail towards the town of River Fork.

'Now, why don't you sit yourself down and have a mug of Bridget's excellent coffee and then tell me what this is about?'

But Jerry was in no state to sit down or to drink coffee. 'I think you should come quickly!' he shouted.

Jack grabbed him by the shoulders to steady him down. 'Tell me what happened, Jerry. Has there been an accident of some kind?'

Jerry shook his head. 'This was no accident,' he sobbed. 'This is cold blooded murder!' Now he did sit down at the table and put his head in his hands and cried like a baby.

Jack looked at Bridget.

'Now, take your time, Jerry, and tell me exactly what's happened and who's been killed.'

Bridget placed a mug of strong coffee in front of Jerry and he drank it back. It seemed to calm him down a little.

Jack put his hand on the man's shoulder. 'OK, tell me who's been killed.'

Jerry looked up at him and shook his head and tried to get the fateful words out. 'Matt Holby and his wife Mary and the two girls. They're all dead!'

Jack's eyes widened. 'You mean the Holbys have been killed?'

'The whole family's dead!' Jerry gasped. 'The whole family, including the girls, all dead!' Jerry looked aghast as though he could still see the murder scene before his eyes.

Jack looked at Bridget and shook his head. 'OK, Jerry, you just sit here and Bridget will pour you a glass of rye to steady your nerves.'

'And you know what,' Jerry said, 'they even tried to burn the place down.'

*

Jack Kincade took down his gun belt and strapped it round his waist. He turned to his wife. 'Look after Jerry, will you, Bridget? I've got to get up to the Holby place.'

He went out to the stable and saddled up Dan, his horse. As he mounted up, he thought of the stranger Tiny had described to him the day before. Tall, tanned as leather, with a scar down his right cheek, and a ring in the form of a snake on the index finger of his right hand. And he had asked directions to the Holby place, too. It was, indeed, highly suspicious.

He rode over to Main Street to visit his friend, Doc Buchanan.

Mrs Buchanan opened the door but didn't look welcoming. She could see from Jack's expression that something serious had happened.

'Has there been an accident?'' she asked.

'No. It seems there might have been a murder,' he replied gravely.

He walked through to the doctor's office. Neither of them shook hands as was their custom. Martin Buchanan picked up on the seriousness of the case immediately.

'There's been a killing,' Jack said. 'At the Holbys' spread. I'm going up there right now to investigate. I'd be obliged if you'd ride along with me, Mart, so we can decide on the causes of death.'

Doc Buchanan nodded and grabbed his medical bag. He wasn't a man to stand idle where injury and death were involved.

As they rode together along the trail to the Holby spread, Jack filled the doctor in on the murder, if indeed it was murder. Then he told Doc Buchanan about the scar-faced

15

man with the snake ring who had asked the way to the Holby spread. Jack Kincade and Doc Buchanan were the best of friends and often discussed their views on crime and politics and anything else of concern. As a healer, Doc Buchanan never carried a gun and he deplored the use of weapons, though he realized that a lawman like his friend Jack needed to carry a gun to maintain the law. Indeed, Jack had needed to draw his gun on numerous occasions but had never had to kill a man so far, and he wasn't at all keen on the idea of shooting anyone.

They saw smoke rising from the Holby spread as they approached. And there was quite a crowd of folk standing around gawping. It's surprising how quickly people were attracted to the scene of a tragedy. Like flies swarming round a pile of horse shit, Jack thought, they buzz in from far and wide.

He and the doctor drew rein in front of the ranch house and dismounted. A man called Greg who seemed to have taken charge came forward.

'Hi there, Sheriff! Hi there, Doc! I'm sure glad you got here.'

The two men dismounted.

'Where are the bodies?' Jack asked.

Greg pointed towards the smouldering building. 'Matt Holby and his wife Mary are on the stoop, and the two girls are way off to the right there. Looks like they were running for their lives when the killer shot them down. We covered the bodies with some gunny sacks to keep the flies off.'

'Has anyone touched the corpses?' Jack asked.

'No, we just made sure they were dead and covered them up.'

Jack and the doctor went over to the stoop to look at the

two bodies. Matt Holby was lying on his back with an expression of horror frozen on his face. His wife Mary was lying closer to the door, on her side as though she had tried to ward off the shot that had blasted her in the head.

'Where are the two girls?' Jack asked Greg.

'They're over to the right there. The killer obviously chased after them and shot them in the back, one in the head and the younger one in the neck.'

Doc Buchanan stayed to examine the adult's bodies and Jack went over to look at the girls who were lying on their front. He stooped to inspect the wounds. Then he took out a note pad and made sketches of the two girls' bodies and wrote a short note to himself, his usual procedure in such circumstances.

'What do you think, Sheriff?' Greg said.

'My guess is they were killed by the gunman as they were running away,' Jack said. 'From the look of the entry wounds, I'd say it was a ball and not a bullet.'

'Those poor little girls,' Greg said. 'At the start of their lives, too. It don't seem right, do it?'

Jack stood up straight. 'It's never right, Greg, whichever way you look at it. Killing people is never right.'

He went back to join the doctor.

'Tell me what you think, Mart,' he said to the doctor.

'Well, one thing's for sure,' Doc Buchanan said. 'Poor Matt took the full blast from a shotgun, and Mary took a ball, probably from an old Cap and Ball. I shan't know for sure until I dig out the ball. We'll have to take the bodies back to town so I can be certain.'

Jack turned his attention to the ranch house. Though somebody had tried to torch it, it was still substantially sound. There had been a lot of smoke but not much fire.

'Now, why should they try to do that?' he asked himself. 'And why didn't they succeed?'

He went back to sketch the two bodies on the stoop so that he would remember in the future.

'OK,' he said to the doc. 'Why don't you ride back to town? I think I must stay right here and see what I can find in the way of evidence.'

After Doc Buchanan had left for town with the four bodies on a buckboard, Jack asked all the rubbernecks loitering round the ranch house what they'd seen and who had been first at the homestead. Although there was some debate, everyone agreed that Jerry, the neighbour, had been the first to arrive. Everyone had his own idea about what had happened and why it had happened, but nobody could be sure.

Jack went back to the cabin and poked around for a bit. Someone had obviously walked in past the bodies and tried to set fire to the place, but why, after killing four people, two of them young girls, would anyone want to set fire to the place?

The idea came to him immediately. It couldn't have been robbery because the stock were still grazing peacefully in the meadow. So it must have been revenge. But who would want revenge against honest homesteaders like Matt Holby and his wife, and those innocent children? And, if you wanted revenge, why kill the man's wife and children, and then try to burn the house down? It would take more than simple revenge for that. It would take something like the rage of a homicidal lunatic!

The sheriff stood on the stoop and looked out in the direction of Silver Spur. And as he looked, a breath of hot

18

wind rose in a twist and he seemed to see a man riding towards him. The man was mounted on a fine piebald horse and he had a face as tanned as well-used leather. And when he spoke, it was in a voice like a growling black bear.

Jack Kincade shook his head and the vision disappeared like a phantom. He checked the Colt Peacemaker in its holster and thought, there might be more in this than meets the eye. I have to find that hombre.

Then he mounted his horse and rode back towards Silver Spur.

CHAPTER TWO

'Like I thought.' Doc Buchanan held up a ball with his tweezers so that it glittered in the light. 'Unless I'm mistaken, an old Navy Cap and Ball. I took that out of Mary Holby's head. And these ...' He pointed to two more balls. '... these came from the head and neck of the two girls. My guess is, the girl who took the shot in the neck took no more than a minute to die and the girl who took it in the head died instantly.'

Jack tried not to grimace.

'As for Matt, he took it full in the chest from a sawn off shotgun.'

'So we have a sawn off shotgun and a Navy Cap and Ball. Are we looking at two killers or one?'

Doc Buchanan considered the matter. 'Could be one but I doubt it. You shoot a man with a shotgun and then draw your Navy Cap and Ball. That seems like a contortion. Why not just use the six shooter for the two of them?'

'And then there are the girls,' Jack speculated. 'They knew what was coming, so they ran away in terror. Maybe there were more than two.'

'My guess is there would be two, but then again, it could

be more.'

Jack nodded thoughtfully. 'And what about motive? You don't just ride on to a property and shoot dead four people without some reason. It doesn't make sense.'

'True,' the doc said. 'But you know what: life doesn't always make sense. Not in my experience, anyway.'

Jack walked across to Bridget's Diner where Jerry was still sitting. He was considerably shaken up but he looked a lot calmer.

Bridget was ready to open the diner and she knew there would be a good many customers since, by now, the whole town knew about the tragic events up at the Holby spread.

Jerry got up from the table. 'I should get back to my spread, Sheriff. The family will need me.'

'Sure,' Jack reassured him. 'I'll ride along with you. But, before that, maybe you could step across to my office and fill me in on the details.'

'What details would they be, Sheriff?'

Jack gave him a reassuring smile. 'Nothing too heavy. Just what you saw and what you remember. It's easy to forget these things with the passing of time, you know.'

'I guess so.' Jerry gave a nervous giggle. 'What d'you want me to say?'

'Just tell me what happened in your own words, and I'll just jot down a few notes.'

'Well, I guess I can do that,' Jerry said. 'Just as long as I'm not under suspicion or anything.'

Jack placed a reassuring hand on the back. 'You tell me what exactly happened, you've got nothing to worry about.'

As they walked across Main Street together to the sheriff's office, Jerry looked right and left as though he feared that someone might jump out and gun him down. But all he saw was Kev Stanley and Tiny Broadhurst and one or two other citizens staring at him from the sidewalk outside the Long Branch Saloon. Tiny Broadhurst took a step forward and raised his hand but Kev Stanley said something quietly and the big man drew back.

When they were in the office, seated across the table from one another, Jack waved his hand. 'OK, just tell me what you saw.'

'OK,' Jerry said. He screwed up his face and tried to remember everything. 'I was working on the farm, cleaning out the pigs and so on, when I heard popping sounds like someone was firing off guns. That didn't worry me none. I thought Matt might be shooting at birds or something. Then I saw the smoke. So I said to Phoebe, my wife, "There's something going on up there. Maybe I should go and take a look see." And Phoebe said, "Yes, maybe you should, but take care in case someone mistakes you for a pigeon!" So I got on my horse and rode over to the Holby place—'

'Hold on, Jerry,' Jack said. 'Now I want you to tell me about those shots. How many did you hear?'

Jerry screwed up his face again. 'Well, maybe six or seven. I can't be sure.'

Jack took a note. 'Then, when you saw the smoke, you rode over to the place.'

'That's right. I thought my neighbour might need help, but I was too late. By the time I got to the spread, they were all dead.' Jerry gave a sob. 'If I'd gotten there a bit sooner I might have been killed myself.'

Jack looked at him. 'Why do you say that?'

22

'Well, it's obvious, ain't it?'

'Well, now, Jerry, let's spell out the obvious, shall we? Are you telling me the killers were still around?'

Jerry took a deep breath. 'I think I interrupted them when they were starting the fire. Otherwise, the whole building might have gone up in flames.'

Jack nodded. 'Did you see anyone?'

'Well, no, I didn't see the killers, but I did hear something.'

Jack stared at him intently. 'Tell me what you heard?'

Jerry paused. 'I heard shouting.'

'How many voices?'

'I can't be sure, at least two. There must have been two because a man doesn't talk to himself unless he's crazy, does he?'

'So you heard shouting. Was it angry shouting or just ordinary shouting?'

Jerry paused again to consider. 'I guess it was like men shouting something like, "Let's get going".'

Jack made another note. 'You sure you didn't see anything?'

Jerry paused again. 'Well, yes, I did see something, I guess. When I heard the shouting, I reined in my hoss and hid behind a stand of cottonwoods. And I caught a glimpse of riders.'

'So you think you did see the killers?'

Jerry shook his head. 'They might have been the killers. I'm not sure. Cause a moment later, Greg and some of the others rode up. So I guess I might have got things a little twisted up in my brain.'

Jack closed his notebook. 'OK, Jerry,' he said. 'Why don't you ride home now and I'll follow you later.'

Jerry sighed with relief. 'I'll do that, Sheriff. Phoebe will be mighty relieved to see me back.'

Jack Kincade walked into the Long Branch Saloon and sat down at the bar. There was a considerable number of drinkers in the saloon and the main topic of conversation was the killing of Matt Holby and his wife and children.

'You got the killers yet, Sheriff?' one wag asked mockingly.

'I'm working on it,' Jack said,

'We're talking about a necktie party,' the wag persisted.

'We sure are,' Tiny Broadhurst added in his somewhat high-pitched tone.

Kev Stanley was behind the bar. 'Can I get you something, Sheriff?'

'You can ask your good woman to take over the bar while I have a few quiet words with you in the back room.'

'Sure, I can do that.' Kev disappeared into the back room and a moment later, his wife came out to tend the bar and Kev beckoned to Jack. As Jack went through to the back room, he felt all eyes in the bar boring into his back. He and Kev sat down together in over-stuffed chairs facing one another.

'So, what can I do for you?' Kev asked the sheriff.

'You can tell me about the stranger who came in yesterday about noon.'

Kev nodded and gave a full description of the man, including the scar on his right cheek and the unusual snakelike ring on his right hand. 'And he was riding a fine piebald horse,' Kev added.

'But he didn't say who he was?'

'He didn't say much at all. He just asked for directions to

24

the Matt Holby place.'

'Is that all?' Jack asked.

'Just that he had an old Navy Cap and Ball in his holster.'

'Are you certain it was a Navy Cap and Ball? Could it have been some other model?'

'I don't think so,' Kev said. 'I've seen a deal of guns in my time and I know one from the other pretty well.'

Jack nodded. 'And you didn't happen to see a sawn off shot gun, did you?'

'The only shotgun I've seen recently is the one I keep under the bar to ward off troublesome customers.'

Jack grinned. 'OK, don't show me in case it goes off by mistake. And thanks for the information.'

Jack Kincade went over to the telegraph office and sent a wire through to the sheriff of River Fork, John Schnell.

Hi, John, I'm looking for a man with a well-tanned face and a scar on his right cheek, wearing a ring like a snake with its tail in its mouth, riding a well-groomed piebald horse. If you see him, please give me a call. But take care because he might be dangerous.'

He said to the operator, 'I'll be in my office or at Bridget's Diner. So if something comes through, you'll know where to find me.'

The operator held up his hand in acknowledgement.

Jack Kincade went over to his wife's diner and sat down at her table. The diner was full and all eyes turned towards him.

'You got the killer yet, Jack?' someone shouted.

'I'm working on it,' Jack replied curtly.

Bridget brought out his dinner and laid it before him. Jack realized he was hungry. You don't think about food when you're working on a case. It wasn't meat pie day, anyway, but who cared.

'You got anything yet?' Bridget asked him quietly.

'Got a description of the possible suspect,' he said. 'It was pretty grizzly up there but I don't want to tell you about that. Thanks for taking care of Jerry. He's not a particularly reliable witness.'

While they were sitting at the table, the telegraph operator came into the diner. He made straight for Jack Kincade and handed him a message.

'This came through from John Schnell.' He handed it over to the sheriff. Jack spread out the paper and read it.

Hi, Jack, I've seen the man you're looking for. He came into town yesterday and picked up supplies. I particularly remember the piebald horse. He didn't hang around town for long. Just lit out. I guess he's set up camp somewhere close. If you ride up, maybe we can track him down together.

Jack wrote a brief message on the paper and handed it to the telegraph operator. 'Send this up to John Schnell, will you, Billy?'

'I sure will, Jack.'

'And another thing: this is law business, and it's strictly confidential. You understand me?'

'I sure do.' The operator gave a cut away salute.

'I won't ask you what that was about,' Bridget said from across the table.

'Please don't,' Jack said with a wink. 'I'll be away for a couple of days.'

'Two days?' Bridget raised her rather delicate eyebrows.

Jack grinned. 'For your information, I'll be riding up to River Fork, but that's an official secret.'

'What shall I tell these people?' she enquired with a smile. 'And what shall I tell the kids?'

'Just say I've gone fishing,' he replied.

'They won't believe it.'

'They won't have to,' he said.

When Jack rode up to the sheriff's office in River Fork some hours later, Sheriff John Schnell came out to greet him. 'Hi, Jack! Come right in. It's been a long time.'

They went into the office and sat down together.

'Any developments?' Jack asked.

'Well, not exactly,' John Schnell said. He was a young, slim guy of German origin who took pride in keeping himself fit, and he took his job as a lawman seriously.

'D'you think we can track him down?' Jack asked.

'Not sure about that. He could be some distance away by now. But I have asked around and he's definitely the man you're looking for. Folks particularly remember that fine horse he was riding. Not just your usual old nag. Maybe he stole it from somewhere.' Jim Daley shrugged his shoulders. 'That's really terrible, the massacre down at the Holby place. Those two little girls an' all. This guy we're talking about could be desperate and dangerous.'

'That's why we have to find him,' Jack said.

Then came a big surprise. As they were talking, there came a sharp rap on the door. Before either of them could make a move, the door opened and the man with the face as tanned as leather and a scar on his right cheek stepped into the office.

John Schnell drew his gun, but Jack Kincade looked at the scar-faced man and saw that he had his hands open in an attitude of peace.

'You mind if I come in, Sheriff?' the man growled.

'Are you giving yourself up?' John Schnell asked him.

'You could put it like that,' the man said, 'but I've come to tell you the truth.' He turned to Jack Kincade. 'You wouldn't be the sheriff of Silver Spur, would you?'

'I'm Jack Kincade,' Jack replied.

The man nodded. 'Mind if I sit down, gentlemen? I feel a little bushed and I didn't sleep a lot last night.'

John Schnell pushed forward a chair. 'Take a seat but before you do so, d'you mind if I check that gun of yours?'

The man reached down to his holster.

'Hold on!' Jack said. 'I think I'll take the gun if you don't mind.'

The man raised his hands and Jack lifted the gun from its holster. It was indeed a Navy Cap and Ball, somewhat lighter than his own Colt Peacemaker. Jack checked that it was loaded and laid it on John Schnell's desk. 'What about the sawn off shotgun? Is that out in your saddle bag?'

The man gave a twisted grin, somewhat distorted by the livid scar on his right cheek. 'Never carry a shotgun. Why d'you ask?'

Jack paused for half a second. 'The reason I ask is that Matt Holby was killed by a blast from a sawn off shotgun some time yesterday.'

The man with the scar made a slight movement as though he might fall and then sat down in the chair John Schnell had offered him.

'Could I ask for a cup of water?' he asked.

'Sure, we've got water,' John Schnell said. He poured

water from a large container. 'It's been boiled only today.' He handed the mug over to the stranger and Jack noticed the stranger's hand trembling slightly as he took a long swig.

'So you're here to tell the truth?' Jack said.

The man shook his head. 'I'm here because I just learned what happened,' he said in a husky voice, despite the water.

'Tell us what you learned,' Jack asked him.

The man looked at him with an expression of slight surprise. 'I learned what happened at the Holby farmstead, the massacre of Matt Holby and his wife Mary and the two girls.' As he spoke his voice became more croaky and Jack could have sworn he was on the verge of tears. Either he was genuinely moved or he was a very accomplished actor.

'So you're here because you heard about the massacre?'

'That's right,' the man said.

Jack cleared his throat. 'Now, sir, how come when you stopped at the Long Branch Saloon in Silver Spur the afternoon before last, that you asked the barman the way to the Matt Holby place?'

The man nodded. 'That's because I thought of visiting the Holby farmstead.'

'So did you go there and kill that family?' Jack asked.

The stranger opened his eyes wide. 'I certainly did not!' he said emphatically. 'If I'd been there in time I might have stopped that dreadful crime.'

'Then, if you didn't stop off at the farmstead, what made you change your mind?'

There was a long pause as the man struggled to get his words together. Jack looked at John Schnell, and frowned and shook his head in disbelief.

The stranger managed to pull himself together. 'I rode on to River Fork because I felt guilty.'

John Schnell said, 'I bet you did.'

Jack shook his head. 'You felt guilty about what?'

'I felt guilty about not visiting them before,' he said.

Jack peered into the man's eyes and saw that he was indeed close to tears. 'OK, so you felt guilty about not visiting them. Why should that be, mister?'

'Because we had lost touch and I was coming to them without a bean to my name.'

Jack felt the dawn of understanding but he wasn't yet sure when the sunrise would come. 'Maybe you should tell us who you are, mister.'

The man gave a twisted grin. 'The name's Snake,' he said.

'Snake's not much of a name, is it?' Jack replied sceptically.

'Well, that's the name I go by.'

'Then what's your real name?'

For the first time, the stranger looked Jack straight in the eye. 'I'm Snake Holby, Matt's younger brother.'

After a long pause, Jack sat down with his hands on the table. He glanced at John Schnell, who looked surprised and then puzzled.

'So you're Matt Holby's brother.'

'Yes, I am,' the man replied.

Jack nodded. 'Why don't you tell us the whole story, Mr Snake Holby?'

John Schnell poured a glass of rye whiskey and pushed it over to the man. Snake Holby raised it and said, 'Thank you, sir. I need this. I feel a little shaky right now.'

Jack Kincade thought again, either this guy is a very good actor or he is indeed in shock.

Snake Holby drank down the whiskey in one gulp. 'Truth is,' he said, 'I'm the black sheep of the family. I had a bad bust up with my brother some years back and I've been running wild ever since. Matt is … or was … a good guy, and I have to admit, I've wasted my life. But now I wanted to sort of make amendments. That's why I decided to visit Matt and sort of patch things up before the Grim Reaper comes down to do his business.'

'You think the Grim Reaper is getting close?' John Schnell asked.

Snake Holby gave a twisted grin. 'I think the Grim Reaper leaned down with his scythe and cut off the wrong brother,' he said.

'Well, that's what some people call fate,' Jack said. 'So you were about to call in on your brother and his family but you changed your mind at the last minute. Is that what you're telling us?'

'That's the truth,' Snake Holby insisted.

'OK,' Jack said. 'Now tell me this, Mr Holby, have you any notion about who might have such a deep grudge against your brother that he would want to commit murder on such a scale?'

Snake Holby looked down at his empty glass and then placed it decisively on the table. He looked Jack straight in the eye. 'I don't know the answer to that, Sheriff, but I intend to find out.'

Jack glanced at John Schnell and John Schnell nodded.

Jack turned to Snake Holby. 'Now I'm going to tell you how things stand, Mr Holby. You and me, we're going to ride back to Silver Spur together, you on your fine piebald horse and me on my quite reliable old nag.'

Snake Holby gave a somewhat lopsided grin. 'Does that

31

mean I'm under arrest, Sheriff?'

'If you ride willingly, that won't be necessary,' Jack said. 'Let's just say we have to clear up this mystery as soon as possible.'

'That's what I want as well,' Snake Holby said.

Jack Kincade thanked John Schnell for his hospitality and soon he and Snake Holby were on the trail together, riding towards Silver Spur. Jack had stuck Snake Holby's Navy Cap and ball through his belt. Snake Holby rode a little ahead of Jack but not too far.

'I have something to ask you, Sheriff,' Snake Holby said.

'Ask away,' Jack answered laconically.

'On the way, can we stop off at my brother's farmstead?'

'Why would that be?' Jack asked him.

'I just want to see where he lived and where the murders took place. I might pick up evidence on who might have killed them and why it happened.'

That seemed reasonable enough. 'We can do that,' Jack agreed.

When they rode up to the spread, Jack felt a strange creepy feeling in his spine. The whole place seemed desolate and there wasn't a soul in sight. Even the stock had been driven off, probably by Greg, Jack surmised.

They dismounted and Jack showed Snake where the bodies had been found. Snake stood with his battered Stetson in his hand, looking down at the spot where his brother had died and Jack saw that there was still blood on the stoop.

'Just too late,' Snake muttered to himself.

He went up onto the stoop and then on into the cabin

itself. It was quite modest in size and Matt had built most of it himself with a little help from his friends.

'Why in tarnation did they try to burn the place down?' he asked helplessly.

'Your guess is as good as mine,' Jack replied. He had been watching Snake closely and was coming to the conclusion that he wasn't such a good actor after all. 'So you haven't been here before?' he asked.

'Never before,' Snake said. 'Now I wish I had. Those poor girls, too, just at the start of their lives.' He turned to Jack. 'Where have they laid the bodies?'

Jack told him that Matt and his wife and the two girls were at the funeral director's in Silver Spur waiting to be buried.

'That's where I must go next,' Snake said. 'I need to look at those dead faces.'

'I guess that can be arranged,' Jack said.

They rode into Silver Spur in the heat of the afternoon. There was hardly a soul about but Jack knew very well that folk would be watching. You can't ride into a town like Silver Spur without being observed. He took Snake Holby straight to the funeral director's. The funeral director had been busy with his assistant making pine coffins and he appeared wearing a yellowish apron. He looked at Snake but asked no questions.

'I'm glad you're here, Sheriff. I've been wondering when we can put these good people in the ground.'

'Quite soon,' Jack replied. 'Maybe tomorrow or the next day. We just want to take a look at their faces before you screw the lids down.' Though he sounded nonchalant he was deeply moved. But as a lawman he tried not to show it.

33

They went through to what the funeral director called 'The Funeral Parlour' which, despite the heat outside, the director managed to keep reasonably cool.

'Over here.' The funeral director led them through to the four open coffins. Jack caught the stench of death and stepped aside. Snake approached the coffins and went from one to the other, looking down at the dead faces and muttering to himself.

'Yes, that's Matt,' he muttered. 'So it's come to this. I'm sorry, Matt. I'm deeply sorry.' He looked closely at his brother's corpse and then moved on to Mary's body. 'I'm sorry they did this to you.' He turned away and said to Jack, 'I won't look at the girls. This is enough. Why did I let this happen? Can you answer that, Sheriff?'

Jack had no idea how to answer. He turned to the funeral director. 'I'll see the priest and we'll have the burials as soon as possible.'

Out on Main Street, Snake looked like a broken man. Under his deep tan his face was ash grey.

'What happens now?' he asked Jack.

'What happens now is I lock you up in the jail for your own protection,' Jack said. 'The folk in this town were mighty fond of your brother and they will want revenge against the man who killed him.'

'But I need to find those killers and bring them to justice,' Snake protested.

'That's my job, Mr Holby,' Jack explained, 'and I want those killers just as much as you do. In the meantime, we have to make sure you're safe. I'll have my wife Bridget bring you over a plate of food and I can assure you, you won't be disappointed.'

CHAPTER THREE

After Jack had locked Snake up in the town jail, he took the two horses to the stable so they could rest up and feed. But Jack was uneasy. He was trying to get his head round the recent happenings and it wasn't easy. He wanted to talk things over with the two people he trusted most in the world, his wife Bridget and Doc Buchanan.

As he walked back across Main Street towards Bridget's Diner, he encountered a whole bunch of men, among them Tiny Broadhurst.

'See you got your man, Jack!' Tiny crowed. 'I recognized him as soon as you rode into town. That was mighty fine work, Sheriff. You should get a medal for that.'

'Thanks, Tiny, but I don't go for medals. According to legend, you cleaned them all out in the late war.'

That caused a ripple of laughter among the men and one or two jeered. Jack sensed an edge of menace in some of the voices.

'Why don't you boys go back to work? I've got a lot to think about.'

'Just as long as we get justice for that terrible crime,' one of the men shouted.

'You'll get justice soon enough,' Jack said. 'That's what my job is about.'

As he walked on to Bridget's Diner, the jeering and the grumbling continued like the ripple of water as you approached the rapids.

Bridget's Diner was quite busy. Bridget was serving customers but her assistant Anne-Marie was perfectly competent and the assistant chef knew his business. So Jack and Bridget went through to the back room to talk.

'They tell me you've got the man with the scarred face in the calaboose,' Bridget said.

'Locked him up for his own safety,' Jack told her.

'You mean he's in danger?'

'Oh, he's in danger all right. Most people in Silver Spur have already made up their minds he's guilty, and it's like there's an ugly storm brewing on the horizon. Most folk really liked the Holbys and they're thirsty for revenge.'

'Well, that's understandable,' Bridget said. 'The Holbys were good people. But is the scar faced man the killer? That's what I wonder.'

Jack looked at her sideways. 'Let me tell you something. The guy with the scar claims to be Matt Holby's brother. Says he was on his way to call in on the Holbys but changed his mind at the last minute and rode on to River Fork instead.'

'So he claims to be Matt's brother!' Bridget said in surprise.

'That's what he says.'

'D'you believe him?'

Jack told her how he had taken Snake Holby to the Holby farm and then to the funeral parlour to view the corpses. 'He looked real sick and I saw tears welling up in his eyes.'

'That's strange!' Bridget said. 'So do you believe him?'

'Well, either he's the greatest actor on this side of the fish pond, or he's telling the truth. I told him I'd have you or Anne-Marie take a platter of food over to him before he drops dead of hunger. Can you do that for me?'

'Sure thing.'

But before Bridget could make a move, the door swung open to reveal Doc Martin Buchanan. 'Good afternoon, good people!' the doctor greeted them.

'Hi, Mart!' Jack said. 'I'm glad you're here. I need to tap into your brain somewhat.'

'Ouch!' the doctor said. 'That sounds painful. I don't have much to spare. But I came over to warn you. There's a storm blowing in from River Fork and it's about to collide with another storm cloud from Silver Spur.'

'What are you talking about, my friend?' Jack asked him.

'I'm talking about trouble,' the doc said. 'It seems that some of the citizens from River Fork have made up their minds you've got the Holby killer and they mean to take the law into their own hands. I heard one of them say they'd string him up outside the jail as soon as they've busted him out.'

Jack was on his feet immediately. 'I'll be back!' he said to Bridget.

He walked right through the diner and on into Main Street. He looked across and saw there was a whole crowd of men and even a few women outside his office, maybe as many as thirty.

One of the men, a big beefy fellow, well known as a braggart in River Fork stepped forward. 'Glad you're here, Sheriff,' he said. 'We've ridden down here as a matter of business.'

'What business would that be?' Jack asked him.

'The justice of the frontier,' the burly man said. 'And justice for those poor folk the killer gunned down. They were good people, those Holbys, and the killer has earned his fate.'

Jack looked at the man and saw he meant business. He was carrying a Winchester and he had a sixgun shooter tucked into his belt.

'Fate speaks in a whisper,' Jack retorted. 'He never shouts. He sort of creeps up on a man.'

The braggart looked puzzled. 'If that's from the Good Book, you're wasting your time, Sheriff. Your prisoner needs a whole lot more than the Good Book to save him. He needs justice and we mean to serve it out.'

The voice of Doc Buchanan spoke out from beside Jack. 'That's from the book of common sense, Alonso, and the book of common sense tells me you've wasted your time riding down from River Fork. Why don't you just take a long drink and a bite to eat and then ride back to where you came from? Don't you have business to attend to up there?'

'My business is my business, Doc,' Alonso said. 'We don't waste our time when it comes to justice. We just look it right in the eye and face up to it.'

'What exactly do you want, Alonso?' Jack asked the braggart.

Alonso raised his head. 'We want what everyone else wants. If you'll just hand over the key to the jail, we can do what needs to be done.'

'That's right,' Tiny Broadhurst crowed. 'What we need is revenge. That's what everyone needs. They say blood cries from the ground and that's what happened in the war.'

'An eye for an eye and a tooth for a tooth,' someone else piped up.

There was another murmur of approval from the crowd which was swelling by the minute. Everyone likes a good standoff and where there is blood involved, especially righteous blood, everyone gets thirsty. It was a bit like Christians being thrown to the lions in Roman times, Jack thought.

'So why don't you just hand over those keys right now?' Alonso challenged as he brought the Winchester round towards Jack.

Jack looked down at the Winchester and shook his head. 'That looks like a threat, Alonso. Put up your gun before I arrest you for menacing an officer of the law.'

Alonso's Winchester didn't waver. 'Just hand over those keys, Sheriff, and go back to the diner to have your dinner. Then we can get on with our intended business.'

'You have no business here,' Doc Buchanan said from beside Jack. 'So why don't you just turn around and go right back to River Fork before you involve yourself in a crime which you will surely regret?'

There was a moment of deadly silence while Alonso considered his options, which were indeed very limited. But as most people in Silver Spur knew, Alonso was as stubborn as a mule and had never been known to turn away at the last moment when he was convinced he was right. Indeed he was a big trouble maker. He had a farm up near River Fork but he spent most of his time drinking and gambling in the saloon while his wife and children survived on a pittance.

'OK, Alonso,' Jack said. 'Let's calm down a little, shall we? You put that gun down and we'll pretend none of this happened.'

'That's a good idea,' Kev Stanley said. 'Why don't you boys pile into the Long Branch Saloon for drinks on the house?

Than we can talk this thing over in a civilized manner.'

That did something to relieve the tension. One man laughed. Another said, 'You bet!' And several of the men moved towards the Long Branch Saloon for free drinks. Jack felt a sudden sense of relief. It might cost Kev a mint of money but nobody could refuse such a generous offer, especially after riding down from River Fork. He looked at Alonso and saw that he was deeply disappointed and angry, but even Alonso could see when his moment had passed. The big man gave him a furious glare.

'We'll settle this matter later,' he said.

'Not if you value your life,' Jack said to himself.

After Main Street had cleared, Jack turned to the doctor and sighed with relief. 'Thanks for your intervention, Mart. It could have been a lot worse.'

Doc Buchanan nodded. 'It isn't over yet. You have to decide what to do next. After those hombres have got themselves tanked up they might be even more determined.'

'What do we do now?' Mart asked Jack.

'What do I do now?' Jack muttered to himself.

'Well, we need to make sure those self-righteous men who never hurt a fly don't lynch that scar faced man, don't we?' Mart replied.

'How can we do that?' Jack asked, but he had already thought of a way. 'I'm going into my office and I'm going to take Snake Holby out through the back way.'

'What then?' the doctor said.

'Then I'm taking him down by the back way to the funeral director's. Walt will shelter the man even if it means hiding him in a coffin. Walt might have a grim trade but he knows injustice when he sees it.'

*

When Jack unlocked the door of the cell, Snake Holby came forward and seized his hand. 'Thanks for that, Sheriff. You saved my life.'

Jack shook his hand free. 'We were lucky, that's all.'

'But I heard it all,' Snake insisted. 'If you and your friends hadn't used your savvy, I'd have been swinging like a sack of corn no more than a hundred paces from here.'

'I don't think corn's the right comparison,' Jack said laconically. 'Men are men and corn is corn. Men eat corn but I've never heard tell of a sheaf of corn eating a man.'

'What do we do now?' Snake asked him with a grin.

'What we do is we go out through the back door and along to the funeral director's place. Walt owes me a favour since I've introduced him to one or two clients in my time as sheriff of Silver Spur. I think you'll be safe there, but you might have to sleep in a coffin. Walt does a fine line in coffins as you've seen. You might even get silver handles.'

'Thanks again,' Snake said.

'Don't thank me, Mr Holby, just don't try to make a break for it. If you do I might just have to shoot you.'

Snake Holby gave Jack a crooked grin. 'I won't let you down, Sheriff. I can promise you that. I just want the chance to track down my brother's killers.'

'Well, that's one thing we're in agreement on,' Jack told him.

Jack went over to Bridget's Diner to finish his dinner but somehow his appetite had slackened.

'What happens now?' Bridget asked him.

'What happens is those knuckle heads will emerge from the saloon either sloshed out of their minds or determined to wreak havoc.'

'Unless Kev Stanley has put knock out drops in their drinks to put them to sleep,' Doc Buchanan suggested.

'That's a real good idea,' Jack responded. 'I wish I'd dreamed it up myself.'

It wasn't long before the rabble rousers emerged from the Long Branch Saloon. Some were shouting, some were singing ribald songs, and Tiny Broadhurst was carrying a gun he discharged into the air several times. Even the bully Alonso was laughing. When he saw Jack standing outside Bridget's Diner with a Colt Peacemaker in his hand, he raised his Winchester and then let it drop to his side.

'You got that key ready, Sheriff?' he bawled.

'That's for me to know,' Jack said quietly. 'You step a foot closer with that Winchester of yours and I'm going to have to lock you up in the jail until you've sobered up.'

'You can't do that,' the man shouted.

'You want to try me?' Jack raised his Colt and levelled it at the man.

Alonso swayed and studied the revolver through bleary eyes. 'You're a two bit criminal lover and you're a disgrace to your calling,' he declared, 'and we're gonna string up your prisoner, ain't we, boys?' But there was no response. The so-called *boys* were all busy puking on the sidewalk or ambling off, trying to find their horses. Someone had the presence of mind to untether Alonso's horse and bring it to him. Then a couple of locals, assisted by Doc Buchanan, hoisted the big man up into the saddle. It was no easy task.

'Now, I suggest you ride out of town if you can stay in the saddle, and don't stop until you get to River Fork where my friend the sheriff will probably arrest you for dangerous riding.'

*

When most of the rowdies had ridden out of town, leaving some of their friends to sleep it off on the sidewalk, Jack went over to the Long Branch Saloon to talk to Kev Stanley. The first person he encountered inside the saloon was Tiny Broadhurst, who had returned for another drink.

'Hi there, Sheriff!' Tiny piped up innocently.

'Where's that gun of yours?' Jack demanded.

Tiny grinned. 'Oh, you mean the way I popped off a couple of rounds into the air?' he said.

'I mean disturbing the peace and endangering the populace,' Jack told him.

'Oh, I was just fooling around, Sheriff.'

'D'you think hanging a man by the neck until he dies is fooling around?' Jack asked him.

'Well, I guess me and some of the boys got sort of carried away,' Tiny said with a high-pitched snigger.

'That fooling around could have had fatal consequences for my prisoner. So I'm placing you under arrest so that you can think about it for a while.'

Jack turned to Kev who was grinning behind the bar. 'Thank you, Kev. You did a very fine job there and I want to thank you. How come you knocked those scallywags out like that?'

'Oh, that was nothing,' Kev responded. 'I just spiked their drinks with raw alcohol and they seemed to like it. An old trick I learned way back.'

'Well, that old trick was certainly useful,' Jack said. 'Maybe I should deputize you next time there's trouble in town.'

Kev was still grinning behind the bar. 'I wouldn't want that, Sheriff. You see, I'm strictly a man of peace.'

*

Tiny Broadhurst was none too pleased about being locked up in the calaboose. He held onto the bars as though he thought he might have the strength to wrench them apart. Yes, he was strong but not quite as strong as Samson!

'This ain't right, Jack. I've always been a good citizen,' he protested.

'Good citizens don't threaten to hang prisoners,' Jack retorted.

'Well then, how come you didn't arrest Alonso and those other guys and lock them up? It was Alonso's idea. We didn't know he was dead serious.'

'You got lucky, Tiny,' Jack said. 'I didn't shoot you, did I? If Alonso hadn't been so drunk, thanks to our amigo Kev, I might have had to shoot him, too. You're a first class gossip, Tiny, and Alonso's a bragging bully. So thank whoever you think might be in charge up there that you got away so lightly.'

Tiny plonked himself down on the bunk with a growl and resigned himself to his fate.

Jack walked up to the funeral parlour where he was met by Walt, the funeral director.

'How's the visitor doing?' Jack asked.

The funeral director shrugged. 'I think he finds it a tad creepy in here.'

'He'd find it good deal creepier if he was swinging at the end of a rope,' Jack said.

'Have those rowdies hightailed it out of town?' Walt asked.

'Those that can still stay in the saddle have vamoosed,' Jack told him.

Walt didn't have time to ask him to elaborate since, at

that moment, Snake Holby appeared on the scene.

'So they've lit out?' Snake said.

'They've vamoosed for the present,' Jack agreed. 'What I'm thinking about is what happens in the future.'

'That's what I'm thinking about, too,' Snake said.

Jack wagged his head and pointed a finger at Snake. 'Now listen up, Mr Snake Holby. You can't stay here because sooner or later those rowdies are going to start baying for your blood again.'

'That's true enough,' Snake agreed.

Jack nodded. 'So I'm going to put a proposition to you.' He turned to the funeral director. 'This is off the record, Walt, but I want you to remember this conversation for the future. You understand me?'

'That's as clear as the nose on your face, Jack.'

'In the meantime, don't breathe a word to anyone about this.'

Jack turned to Snake again. 'Now, Mr Holby, I'm going to ask you to stay here until tomorrow when we'll have the funerals of your kin.'

'I'm sure I can manage that,' Snake said. 'Is that all?'

'No,' Jack said, 'that is far from all. After the funeral, we ride out of town and find out who killed Matt Holby and his wife and children and bring them to justice. That's what we do.'

'You mean just the two of us?'

'That's unless you can't abide my company,' Jack said.

A gleam of light appeared in Snake Holby's eyes. 'Does that mean you believe I'm innocent?' he asked.

'That means together we're going to find out the truth about those murders,' Jack said.

*

The morning of the funerals dawned like fire on the horizon. It would be a hot day, Jack thought. The burial ground was high on a hill, overlooking the town of Silver Spur and the river, and a warm breeze swept up the hill and then on into the wilderness. Earlier there had been a funeral service for the Holbys in the little mission church on the edge of town. Now the priest, an old Jesuit father called Ignatius, stood by the grave and sprinkled holy water over the coffins. There had been very few people in the mission church but there was a large crowd at the grave site.

Jack Kincade stood well back to observe the proceedings. He was determined to make sure nothing unlawful happened to his prisoner Snake Holby.

He noted that very few of the rowdies were present. Most of them were probably nursing huge hangovers. The bully Alonso was also mercifully absent. Even the worst kind of men don't like to behave badly at a funeral. So, if he hadn't fallen off his horse, he was probably back in River Fork being nagged by his long-suffering wife.

Jack saw that there were quite a few of Holby's neighbours in evidence, including Greg and Jerry, the man who had been first on the scene at the Holby Spread. A few of the local kids were present but most them were at school as usual. Stephanie and Gregory were grieving for their friends, the two Holby girls.

Jack had asked Bridget not to attend the funeral but she had insisted on being there. She was standing right beside Jack with Doc Buchanan and his wife Suzanna. Suzanna was a short, fair-haired woman who said very little but knew her own mind. She was a particular friend of Bridget's.

'What do you think?' Mart Buchanan asked Jack.

'What do I think about what?' Jack replied.

'What do you think about life and death?'

Jack grinned. 'I try not to think about it too much unless I have to. I guess we all have to face it in the end and there's no going back when you get there, is there? When you're dead, you're stone cold dead and that's a plain fact.'

'Well, that's quite a profound statement for a man of the law,' the doctor acknowledged with a twinkle in his eye. 'But have you noticed anything in particular about our friend Snake Holby?'

Jack had indeed been observing Snake Holby, and he saw a man standing close to the graveside with his head bowed and his hat in one hand and a handful of soil in the other, and he was scattering soil onto each of the coffins.

'They're all in there together,' Bridget said quietly. 'One grave and four coffins. That's the way it should be, together in death as they were together in life.'

'It shouldn't have been so,' Suzanna Buchanan murmured.

Now a number of people surged forward to drop soil into the grave and Jack moved closer to keep an eye on Snake Holby in case somebody pushed him into the grave or attempted to commit some other offence on his prisoner. But, fortunately, nobody did.

Yet something unexpected did happen. A man whom Jack knew as Hubert Parry sidled up and murmured in his ear. 'Excuse me, Sheriff, after the burial I'd like to have a word with you.'

Jack looked at him and saw an expression of fear and anxiety on his face. Then he saw the man's son, Hubert Junior, standing beside him and he too was looking eager and anxious.

'You have something to tell me?' Jack said.

47

Hubert Parry spoke in a hoarse whisper, so quietly that Jack could scarcely pick up the words. 'My son Hubert Junior here thinks he might know who killed Matt Holby and the family.'

Jack looked at the son who was perhaps fifteen years old, and Hubert Junior gave a slight nod and said, 'Yes, I do, sir.'

Jack turned to his friend, Doc Buchanan. 'Mart, I have to talk to these people. Would you be kind enough to keep an eye on Snake Holby for me?'

'That will be a pleasure, my friend.'

Jack took the man and his son to a small cabin where the grave digger kept tools of his trade and brewed up his coffee. It was the most private place on the burial ground.

'So you think you know who killed the Holby family?' he asked sceptically.

'Yes, I do, sir,' the boy piped up confidently.

'Why haven't you come to me before?'

Hubert Parry Senior intervened. 'That's because we thought we might be in danger, sir,' he said.

'OK,' Jack looked at the boy. 'So tell me what you know.'

Hubert Parry Junior was a bright kid. Jack could see that by the eager look in his eye. And he told his story clearly and precisely.

The Parrys had a farm quite close to the Holbys and on the morning of the murders, the youth had been out looking for a stray cow. He had tracked it down to the creek and was about to rope it and take it back to the farm when he heard riders approaching. So, instead of lassoing the steer, he left it to drink its fill in the creek, and he took cover in a stand of willows close to the bank. As he was crouching close to the creek, three riders rode up and watered their horses in the creek.

'Three, you say?' Jack asked him.

'Yes, sir, there were definitely three. Two of them were young, just a few years older than me, and the third was much older. He had a big bushy beard like Saint Christopher.'

'So,' Jack said, 'what made you think they had anything to do with the murders?'

'Well, sir, that's because I heard what they said.'

Jack looked faintly surprised. 'So tell me what they said.'

The youth glanced towards the door as though he was afraid someone might be listening outside.

'It's all right, son,' Hubert Parry Senior said. 'You can tell the sheriff what you heard. Just speak up honest and clear.'

The boy gave a croaky cough and continued with his story.

'Well, first off one of the younger men said, "Look at that steer there, Hank, it looks kinda lost," and the older man, the one with the beard, said, "You don't need to worry none about that lost steer, son, unless you want to rope it in and have it for your dinner." Then they all laughed and I crouched down in those willows a little closer. It wasn't about the steer, it was about the way they laughed. But when they spoke again, I knew I was right to hide away like that.'

'So what did they say?' Jack asked him.

'Well,' the boy reflected, 'one of the younger men – I think it was the other one – said, "Well, you got what you wanted, Hank," and the older man said, "Revenge is sweet, Justin."'

'Revenge is sweet,' Jack repeated. 'Are you sure he used that word revenge?'

'That's what my boy told me,' Herbert Parry Senior said.

'That was the very word.'

'Yes, sir,' the boy added. 'He said revenge. But that wasn't all. Justin, the younger man said, 'You shot Holby with that scatter gun of yourn and I shot the woman with that Cap and Ball you gave me. But did we have to shoot those two young girls like that? They didn't do nothing, did they?" Then the bearded man Hank, laughed and said, "Dead men tell no tales, my son, and that applies to boys and girls, too. You know that?" "All the same, I didn't like doing it," Justin said. I think it was Justin. It's difficult to remember now.'

Hubert Parry Junior was trembling and Jack put a hand on his shoulder to reassure him. 'You did a fine job remembering all that. Did they say anything else?'

The boy closed his eyes. 'No, that's just about all, sir. After that they just said they were riding north to River Fork. Then they got on their horses and rode away, and I felt relieved I had got away with my skin.'

CHAPTER FOUR

The mourners were now dispersing. Hubert Parry and his son had got on their horses and ridden back to their farm. Jack joined Bridget, Doc Buchanan, Suzanna and Snake Holby at the graveside. Jack saw that Snake Holby had become quite withdrawn and pale under his leathery tan. The others rode ahead and Jack rode close to Snake.

'Listen, Snake,' he said, 'I've received information about the killing of your brother and his family.'

Snake looked surprised. 'You mean you know who the killers are?'

'Not exactly. Did you ever hear of a man called Hank?'

'Hank who?' Snake asked him.

'A man with a big bushy beard like Saint Nicholas or Saint Christopher,' Jack said.

'There are lots of bearded men called Hank.'

'That's true.' Jack nodded. 'I have a witness who says he heard this Hank boasting about how he had killed your brother. And there were two younger men with him. One went by the name of Justin. Does that tinkle a bell in your brain?'

Snake frowned and shook his head. 'Are you dangling

51

something like a carrot in front of me, Sheriff?'

Jack grinned. 'I'm just trying to establish the truth, Snake. That's all I'm doing. And one part of the truth I'm starting to catch a glimpse of is …'

Snake narrowed his eyes. 'And what might that be, Sheriff?'

'That might be that, unless you hired those killers yourself, you're innocent of your brother's blood,' Jack said.

Snake gave a creased up smile. 'So now you believe my story?' he asked.

'I'm inclined to, Snake … I'm inclined to.'

'Then maybe you'll tell me what happens next and what you're going to do about it.'

Jack nodded and said, 'I'm thinking on that, Mr Holby. But I will tell you one thing, Mr Holby. I'm going to trust you and I'm not about to lock you up in the jail again.'

'Well, thanks for that, Sheriff. It's not too comfortable in that lock up of yours. And the thought of being strung up for a crime I didn't commit doesn't appeal too much, either.'

'Well, I'm glad it isn't too snug in there,' Jack said. 'We don't want the hoodlums to get a taste for the place. So, instead, you will become a guest in Bridget's Diner.'

Snake raised his eyebrows. 'How come?'

'For your own protection, Mr Holby,' Jack told him. 'I don't want those rowdies trying to lynch you again, because I have other plans. There's a very comfortable room above Bridget's Diner and you can rest and even have a bath and freshen up. It'll be like staying in the Grand Hotel, but only for one night. So make the best of it.' He turned to Snake. 'But if you try anything stupid I might have to shoot you after all.'

*

Jack went over to his office where Tiny Broadhurst was still languishing in the jail. Tiny was lounging on the bunk, thinking of all the stories he might invent to tell his friends about how he had almost been lynched and how the sheriff had locked him up for his own protection.

When Jack turned the key in the lock, Tiny sprang up with surprising agility for such a big man. 'So!' he exclaimed. 'Did that scar faced hombre get his just desserts?'

'Not yet,' Jack replied. 'We're still working on it.'

'And I missed the funerals,' Tiny complained. 'There's nothing I like so much as a good funeral. You see a lot of interesting things at a good funeral. It's all about reading the human mind, you know.'

'Well, I'm sorry you missed your entertainment for the day. Why don't you just wander down to the Long Branch Saloon and get yourself a drink to make up for your hours of incarceration?'

'You mean I'm free?'

'You're free just as long as you don't try to get anybody else lynched. And I'd advise you not to open your mouth and blabber too much about it in case you swallow a fly or something a whole lot bigger.'

Jack walked over to Doc Buchanan's office to discuss matters. He told Mart Buchanan all he had heard from the young boy, Hubert Parry.

The doctor's eyes widened. 'I know the boy, known him since he was a babe in arms. In fact, I helped bring him into the world and I tended his mother in her last illness.'

'Didn't she die in childbirth?' Jack asked.

'Yes, and we couldn't save the child, either,' the doctor

said. 'A sad case but unfortunately, one in so many.' He gave Jack a quizzical look. 'So what do you intend to do about this new evidence?'

'Well, Mart, I obviously need to follow up on it if I'm going to catch those killers.'

'Indeed,' Doc Buchanan agreed. 'But what about this guy Snake who claims to be Matt Holby's brother?'

'I'm still thinking on that,' Jack said.

The doctor was about to ask another question but, at that moment, Suzanna opened the door and peeped in. 'Sorry to interrupt your consultation, gentlemen,' she said, 'but young Jeremiah is out here asking to see Mr Kincade.'

'Mister,' Jack said. 'When people call me mister, I know it must be something serious.' He got up and went to the outer office. 'What is it, Jeremiah?' he asked the young man.

'Mr Vickery sent me,' the youth said. 'He said if you can spare a minute, would you please step up to his office. He thinks there's something you should know.'

Jack walked up to the lawyer's office and the youth marched swiftly ahead. Jeremiah hoped to be a lawyer himself someday, just like Abraham Lincoln and his master Larby Vickery.

When Jack walked into the lawyer's office, Larby Vickery rose from behind his desk and stretched out his hand in greeting.

'Ah, Mr Kincade, I'm delighted to see you. Please sit yourself down.' He turned to young Jeremiah. 'That will be all, Shuttleworth. You can resume your work.'

The youth said, 'Certainly, Mr Vickery.' And he bowed himself out.

'Well, I'm here at your request, Mr Vickery,' Jack said with a hint of irony.

The lawyer acknowledged the irony with a slight nod. He had encountered Jack's sense of the ridiculous on more than one occasion. Like many lawyers he was inclined to take life seriously, especially when it came to money matters and the law.

'As you may know, Mr Kincade, I have represented Mr Holby in legal matters since he first bought the farm some ten years ago.'

Jack leaned back and listened. 'I haven't given much thought to that,' he admitted, 'and I didn't think Mr Holby had any legal matters to speak of.'

Larby Vickery scratched the side of his bulbous nose. 'Well, that's true,' he reflected. 'But there's one thing I have to tell you.' He looked up at some spot to the right of Jack's shoulder. 'You see, Mr Matthew Holby left a will and I have it here in my possession.' He placed his hand on a document on his desk.

Jack gave a faint smile. 'I don't think that's my concern, not unless it has some connection with his unfortunate death.'

The lawyer puckered his brow in thought. 'That may or may not be true, Mr Kincade,' he said.

Jack leaned forward. 'There's something I have to tell you, Mr Vickery. You must have heard that I have a man in custody.'

'Yes, I have heard that,' the lawyer admitted. Since he kept himself informed about everything that happened in town, Jack knew he must know about the man called Snake.

'Well, there's one thing you might not know and that's that the man called Snake is Snake Holby.'

'Snake Holby!' Vickery said in surprise.

Jack grinned. It was always good to give a lawyer a

surprise. 'Snake Holby claims to be Matt Holby's younger brother.'

Jack could almost hear the wheels in Vickery's mind churning round.

'So,' Jack added, 'if you've got the Holby will on your desk there, maybe he's the one you should be reading it to.'

The wheels in Vickery's mind kept turning for a while. 'Well now, Sheriff, I have something to tell you that might change the situation completely.'

'Is that so?'

Vickery's hand rested on the will for a moment. 'Matt Holby was a widower. He was married to another woman before he married Mary.'

'A widower,' Jack said. 'You mean his former wife died?'

Vickery was guarded. 'I don't know about his first wife, Mr Kincade. She might be dead and she might be still alive. But I do know one thing: he married Mary in the church right here in town. Maybe that was before your time.'

That had been before Jack took the sheriff's badge of office. 'So what you're telling me, Mr Vickery, is that Matt Holby might have married Mary bigamously?'

'I have no information on that, Mr Kincade. But ...' He leaned forward intently. '... I can tell you one thing and that is that Matt Holby had a son by that first marriage.'

'Did he now?' Jack reflected.

'His name is Edward Joe Holby. '

'Edward Joe Holby,' Jack said quietly. 'So, is he still around?'

Vickery gave a conspiratorial smile. 'Not only is he still around, he's mentioned in Matt Holby's will as a beneficiary.'

'A beneficiary,' Jack said to himself.

'That means he will inherit Matt Holby's property now that the two daughters and his wife are deceased.'

Jack ran his hand over his stubbly jaw. 'So, what do you know about this son Edward Joe Holby?'

Vickery was still smiling like a man who has a pop up clown hidden in a box under his desk. 'Edward Joe Holby lives in Missouri. I'm not free to disclose his address but I've been in touch with him and right now he's on his way here.'

'You mean he's coming to Silver Spur?'

'He'll be arriving in the next day or two.'

When Jack left the lawyer's office, he was in something of a quandary. He felt like a swimmer who suddenly realizes he was way out of his depth. Sink or swim, he said to himself as he walked down to Bridget's Diner.

'What did that old skinflint want with you?' Bridget asked him.

'Larby Vickery put the cat right into the pigeon house,' Jack said, 'and it's ruffling the feathers in my mind.' He told Bridget everything the lawyer had said.

'So there's a lot more to Matt Holby than we thought there was?' she speculated.

'There could be a whole pack of cards more,' he agreed. 'But where's Snake Holby right now?'

'He's out back reading the newsheets,' she said.

Jack went out onto the lot and saw Snake Holby with a copy of the local newspaper spread before him. 'So, you're still here, Mr Holby.'

Snake Holby looked up. 'Gave you my word, didn't I?'

Jack sat down beside him on the step. 'How much do you know about your brother?' he asked.

Snake squinted round at him. 'What do you mean, what

do I know? He was my brother, that's all. He was more than ten years older than me. He was the steady one of the family and I was the wild one. Like I told you earlier, I hardly knew him at all.'

'Did you know he had two families?'

'What do you mean, two families?'

'Like he married earlier and had a son called Edward Joe Holby.'

Snake stared ahead and then started to shake. Jack didn't know whether he was shaking with grief or with laughter and then decided it must be laughter. 'Well, that's a real turn around. So my steady brother Matt had two wives. Is his first wife still alive?'

'I have no information on that,' Jack said. 'But I understand from the lawyer Larby Vickery that your nephew Edward Joe is a beneficiary in his father's will now the two girls are dead.'

'Is that so?' Snake turned the whole thing over in his mind. 'But that doesn't make a heap of difference to me, does it, Mr Kincade?'

'That's for you to decide,' Jack said. 'And you'd better decide quickly because Edward Joe is on his way to Silver Spur right now.'

Snake grinned and the scar on his right cheek seemed to grin with him; it wasn't a pretty sight. 'So what do we do about those killers?' he asked Jack.

Jack thought on the matter. 'Sooner or later, I have to ride to River Fork and take those scaramouches into custody,' he said.

Snake was still grinning. 'That won't be easy. Those scaramouches will shoot you as good as look at you. In which case you need another gun to guard your back.'

'Which gun would you recommend?'

'That would be my gun, Mr Kincade. It's the most reliable gun you're likely to get. And I have good reason to help you arrest those killers. They say blood is thicker than water and I'm beginning to see reason in that. You might even deputize me to make it legitimate.'

Jack gave him a level look. 'I don't want any more revenge killings in Silver Spur,' he said.

'I just want those men who killed my kin to be brought to justice one way or the other,' Snake said. 'And I can tell you this: you couldn't have a better gun by your side.'

Jack was still looking Snake in the eye. 'I don't know a whole lot about you, Snake. How do I know you are who you claim to be?'

'Like I told you, Mr Kincade, I'm the wild boy in the pack. How d'you think I got this scar on my face? It wasn't from wrestling with a bear, I can tell you that. It was from wrestling with a man who tried to stab me dead in a bar in Kansas. They took me to hospital and stitched me up real good as you can see.'

'What happened to the man who attempted to stab you?'

'I had to shoot him. It was a matter of kill or die. So I killed him stone dead. Nobody thanked me but I think I rid the community of a scrounger who was no better than a skunk. So I regarded it as a duty. They should have given me a reward for what I did. Instead they locked me up in the calaboose for a while. Luckily the judge saw it as self-defence, so they set me free. Otherwise I might have swung from on high. So you see this wasn't the first time I had to use my shooter.'

'What about that fine snake ring of yours?'

'Well, I just took it off the hombre's finger. Thought it

59

was the best reward I would ever have, and the sheriff never knew about it.'

'Was he the only man you ever killed?'

Snake grinned again. 'I don't know, Sheriff, I never keep count.'

Jack reflected on the merits of Snake's case. 'I'll send a wire up to River Fork,' he said. 'John Schnell, the sheriff, will tell me whether those three scallywags have hit town yet. He should be warned, anyway. They might be intent on more murder and mayhem up there.'

Jack walked over to the telegraph office and sent a message to his friend, the sheriff of River Fork, describing the three men Hubert Parry had talked about. He gave Schnell as detailed a description as possible and warned the sheriff that they might be extremely dangerous.

Next morning Jack and Snake were at the Wells Fargo Depot when the stage rolled in. And Larby Vickery was waiting there, too. The stage was no more than twenty minutes late which was early since you never knew what you might encounter on the way. The driver prided himself on always being on time, plus or minus half an hour or so. He called in on the railway depot closest to Silver Spur as there was no rail connection to Silver Spur.

That day there were nine passengers on the stage, plus baggage, and the last passenger to disembark was a man in his early twenties dressed in a brown bowler hat and town clothes, a man one would scarcely associate with frontier life, and probably a man who would be close to the lawyer Larby Vickery's heart. Larby Vickery stepped forward immediately and offered his hand. 'You must be Mr Edward Joe Holby.'

'I am indeed,' the young man admitted with a smile. He was obviously a young man with a promising future, and he didn't resemble his uncle Snake Holby in the least.

'I'm so sorry you've come at such a sad time, Mr Holby,' the lawyer said ingratiatingly.

'It's a pity I missed the funeral,' Edward Joe said. 'But the truth is I never knew my father.'

Larby Vickery turned to Snake Holby. 'And this is your father's brother, another Mr Holby.'

The young man looked at Snake appraisingly. 'So you must be my uncle?' he said.

'I guess I must be,' Snake agreed coolly.

Larby Vickery then turned to Jack. 'And this is Sheriff Jack Kincade who is investigating the sad case of your father's murder.'

Jack took Edward Joe's hand which was as limp and cold as a dead fish. 'I've been told I'm the beneficiary,' the young man said.

'That's what Mr Vickery tells us,' Jack replied.

'What about the murders? Have you made an arrest yet?'

'I'm working on it,' Jack said. 'It's a complicated case, and as yet we don't have a motive.'

'Well, maybe I can help on that,' the young man said. Despite his limp handshake he obviously didn't lack confidence. 'But first I need somewhere to lay down my head for the night.'

'Well, there are only two places I would recommend in Silver Spur,' Larby Vickery said. 'One is Bridget's Diner and the other is the Long Branch Saloon.'

'Then maybe you'll be kind enough to take me to Bridget's Diner. It sounds just the place for me.'

The young man had a substantial amount of baggage

and it was obvious he intended to stay in Silver Spur, which struck Jack as strange. Larby Vickery had his understudy, the youthful Jeremiah Shuttleworth, load the bags on to a trolley and wheel them down to Bridget's Diner.

Jack thought to himself, this young man Edward Joe is a bit of a pain in the arse but obviously Larby Vickery thinks he's going to be rich, yet on what I don't yet know; his father Matt Holby hadn't more than two beans to rub together so what can his inheritance be worth?

After Edward Joe Holby had been settled in at Bridget's Diner, Jack went over to the telegraph office and, sure enough, a message had come through from his friend, the Sheriff of River Fork.

Howdy, Jack. I've asked around like you said in your message and there have been three men answering to your description in the town in the last few days. The one with the beard seemed to be in charge. The two younger men were like his sons. I heard this morning that they've now moved on but I don't know where to. Give me a call when you can. John Schnell, Sheriff of River Fork.

Next morning, young Edward Joe Holby was as bright as a button on the tunic of a bombardier. After a hearty breakfast which he took with his uncle Snake, he announced his intentions for the day. First, he would go over to Larby Vickery's office to read his father's will. Then he would go to the bank to sign the necessary documents and find out how much he had inherited. After that, he would purchase a gun.

'Why don't you step across to Mr Vickery's establishment for the reading of the will?' he asked Snake Holby.

'You don't need me,' Snake answered defensively.

'Of course I need you. You're my father's brother and you have a right to know what's in the will.'

'Well, we know you inherit the farm for what it's worth,' Snake said grudgingly. 'But I will step across if that's what you want.'

'And I think you should come, too,' Edward Joe told Jack.

Jack nodded. 'If you want me to.'

They went across to the lawyer's office. Larby Vickery spread the paper on his desk and donned his gold-rimmed spectacles. He could see perfectly well without them but they gave him dignity and never failed to impress his clients. He read the will somewhat theatrically while the others listened in silence.

'So,' he announced at the end of his performance, 'Mr Edward Joseph Holby, you have inherited the Holby farm.'

'Which is just a burned out shell,' Snake said.

Larby Vickery raised a portentous finger. 'We mustn't forget the money, must we, Mr Holby?'

'But I thought my brother didn't have a bean to his name,' Snake said.

'Well,' Larby Vickery beamed, 'I think you're in for a surprise, gentlemen.' He got up from behind his desk like one of the gods of Olympus. 'I've made an appointment with Mr Clarkson, the bank manager and we'll walk up to the bank, if you please, and he will enlighten you on the matter.'

Mr Clarkson, the bank manager, seemed delighted to see them. He invited them into his inner sanctum and asked them to take seats. 'Bring in the Holby strong box,' he ordered one of his clerks.

The clerk disappeared and, a few minutes later, returned

with an assistant carrying a heavy leather-bound box.

Snake Holby glanced at Jack and raised an eyebrow but Jack didn't respond. The clerks laid the leather bound box on the manager's desk.

'Perhaps you'll be kind enough to sign for this, Mr Holby,' Larby Vickery said to Edward Joe Holby.

Edward Joe Holby took the offered pen and signed for the box. He unlocked the box and looked inside. 'What's this?' he asked in astonishment.

'I believe you'll find it's gold, Mr Holby, though there might be some silver, too.'

Edward Joe Holby opened his mouth in astonishment and even Jack Kincade raised an eyebrow.

'How much is there?' Edward Joe asked.

'I don't know, sir. We haven't counted it and Mr Holby never said. We've just kept it in the safe, as he instructed.'

'Well, I'll be goldarned!' the young man said.

The bank manager coughed discreetly. 'Then there's the matter of the balance, Mr Holby.'

'The balance! What balance?' Edward Joe asked.

'The late Mr Matthew Holby's account. I think you'll find there's a considerable sum in the account and that now comes to you, of course.'

It appeared to take several minutes for Edward Joe's good fortune to sink in. Then he turned to his uncle and Jack Kincade and said, 'Gentlemen, you must join me in a drink to my good fortune, though we must also remember the father I never knew and drink to him and his family, too.'

They marched down to the Long Branch Saloon. Edward Joe ordered whiskies all round, even for those who had been drinking in the saloon before he arrived. Much to his astonishment and delight, Tiny Broadhurst was included. Kev Stanley looked at Jack Kincade and asked him if Christmas had arrived early this year.

Jack was somewhat preoccupied. He was still thinking about Matt Holby and the money and gold he had stashed away in the bank. How had he come by it? And did his wife Mary know about it? And if not, why not? The hardworking man of the soil suddenly transformed chameleon-like before his eyes. He was sitting next to Snake Holby and Snake was grinning at him like a devil who has suddenly spotted a likely victim.

'You know what I'm thinking?' Snake said quietly.

'I know you're about to tell me,' Jack replied.

Snake screwed up his face, a clear indication he was thinking hard. 'I'm thinking that brother of mine wasn't the good boy after all. You don't accumulate all that gold and all those dollars by just sitting there and doing nothing, do you?'

'I guess not,' Jack said.

'No, you're right,' Snake continued, 'especially when your good woman is busy scratching out a living on the farm and she knows nothing about it. You know what that adds up to, don't you?'

'To me, it adds up like a double life,' Jack admitted.

'And that must connect with those murders,' Snake went on speculating. 'You know what I'm thinking, Mr Kincade?'

'I'm no mind reader, Snake, but I would say you're thinking those murders were an act of revenge like the boy told us. Your brother was no halo-wearing saint and he deceived his wife. What he meant to do with all those green backs and gold and silver we may never know.'

'Well now, this nephew of mine has his inheritance and

we shall soon see which way the cookie crumbles.'

At that moment, Edward Joe rose to his feet and held up a glass. 'Gentlemen,' he said in a loud inebriated voice, 'I want to propose a toast. Here's to my father and his wife and children who are no longer with us. And here's to us as we uncover the truth about how and why they were murdered!'

CHAPTER FIVE

'This is getting more and more weird,' Jack said to his friend Doc Buchanan. 'Give me your slant on it, Mart.'

'"Beware of Greeks bearing gifts",' Doc Buchanan quoted cryptically.

'Well, that might be sound advice,' Jack said, 'but I don't see quite how it fits in here.'

'It might not be a precise fit,' the doctor agreed, 'but it will do pretty well as a starting point. That young dandy son of Holby orders drinks all round. That's the gift part. But he comes all the way from Missouri by the railroad with his full baggage, obviously expecting to stay. That's the Greeks coming from afar part.'

'I think I'm with you on that,' Jack said. 'Perhaps you'll push me along the rails a little further.'

'The next part is somewhat less clear,' Doc Buchanan admitted, 'Except for this: when the Greeks arrive, they always expect something in return for their pains and our friend Edward Joseph Holby hits the jackpot and sweeps the board.'

'Well, the Greek story is interesting and profound I'm sure, my friend, but it still doesn't make a lot of sense to me.'

'Maybe and maybe not, but tell me in what way it doesn't make sense.'

'It doesn't make sense because right now, Edward Joe is out in the yard honing his shooting skills with the Smith and Wesson revolver he just bought. And his uncle Snake is out there encouraging him.'

'That does add up to a complication,' Doc Buchanan admitted. 'But what does it mean?'

'It means that this guy Edward Joe is determined to find his father's killers and bring them to justice or shoot them down in the process.'

'That's a pretty big ambition for a city slicker who never toted a gun in his life before,' the doctor said.

'It surely is,' Jack agreed.

Before they could go over to Bridget's Diner to check out the gun-toting nephew, a boy arrived from the telegraph office. 'The boss says can you step over to the office, Sheriff Kincade?' the boy said with lick-spittle politeness.

'Where's it from?' Jack enquired.

'I think it came in from River Fork,' the boy said. 'I think it's from the sheriff up there.'

Jack and Doc Buchanan got up from their seats. Jack had a feeling in his bones that the message must be of vital importance. So he walked right up to the Telegraph Office and the telegraph operator handed him the message.

Howdy, Jack! There's been a new development up here at River Fork. One of those three men you described in your last message has shown up right here on my doorstep. Says his name's Aubrey Appleton. Claims to be one of the gang that killed the Holby family. Says he didn't do any of the shooting himself and he wants to come clean about the whole thing.

Right now, I'm holding him in the town jail. But he's a real hot potato. So I'd be glad to drop him as soon as maybe. Please advise. John Schnell.

'Will there be any reply?' the telegraph officer asked.

Jack took a pencil and drafted a reply.

Hi, John! Thanks for your message. Please hold the hot potato for a bit longer. I'll ride up just as soon as I can to relieve you of his company. But don't take any chances, amigo. We're in a dangerous and puzzling situation here. Jack.

Jack returned to Doc Buchanan's office but the doctor was busy with a patient who had a bad attack of the croup. So he went back to Bridget's Diner to confer with his wife. Bridget wasn't altogether sympathetic.

'What are you getting yourself into here, Jack?' she asked.

'I won't know the answer to that question until I look into it a lot deeper,' he answered.

'I guess that means you're going to ride up to River Fork,' she said.

'Well, I guess I have to, because River Fork isn't going to come to me, is it?'

Bridget pursed her lips and nodded. She's still a very fine woman, Jack thought. She was beautiful when I married her and she's just as beautiful now. She's got a brain in her head, too, which is some bonus!

'Pity I can't come with you.' Bridget said, 'but I have to look after the kids and they're real upset after the death of their friends. But take good care of yourself. You're likely to

69

act a little hastily when you're on your own.'

'Well, that's as maybe, but I don't think I shall be on my own, anyway.'

Bridget looked somewhat startled. 'Then, who will you taking with you?'

Jack looked a little uneasy. 'I think I must take Matt Holby's brother Snake and Edward Joe, Matt's son,' he admitted.

Bridget's eyes widened even more. 'Well, that's a damned foolish notion, Jack.'

'Why so?' he asked.

'For two reasons,' she responded. 'First, Snake Holby is about as reliable as a rattlesnake on a hot day, and second because Edward Joe Holby hasn't learned to shoot straight yet.'

'I believe he's doing his best to learn,' Jack retorted.

Bridget gave a snort. 'The trouble with you, Jack, is you're far too trusting.'

Jack grinned. 'Maybe that's why I was elected sheriff of Silver Spur,' he said ironically.

They went out through the diner to find Snake and Edward Joe talking together with apparent amity.

'So, there's nothing to it,' Snake was saying. 'You just keep yourself steady. You level your shooting piece and hold your breath and fire. But don't snatch at the trigger. That way you'll most likely miss your target.'

'I think I'm getting the hang of it,' Edward Joe said amiably as he cradled the Smith and Wesson in the palm of his hand.

Snake grinned in his usual unattractive way. 'We might have wasted a little ammunition here, but you're making good progress. Your hand is steady and you've got a good eye. But like I said, you've bought yourself a pea shooter here. Thirty-two calibre. Something heavier would be better, a .44 or a .45. I've seen a man with a .45 knock another man back so far it was like a high wind blasting him right off his feet. And he didn't get up again, either!' Snake gave an unpleasant sounding chuckle.

'So you've been practising?' Jack intervened.

'There wasn't much else to do, was there?' Snake said.

'Well, there could be from now on,' Jack told him. He sat down on the stoop and told them about the message from River Fork. As he did so he watched both men with keen interest.

'So what's our next move?' Snake asked.

'Well, I know what my next move is,' Jack said. 'I have to ride up to River Fork come sunup tomorrow. I figure my friend John Schnell might be in deep shit up there and I have a responsibility to get right to the bottom of this mystery.' He saw that both Snake and Edward Joe were scrutinizing him closely. It occurred to him as it had earlier that each of them might be implicated in the Holby murders, though he had learned to trust Snake. But why had Edward Joe inherited so much wealth from his father, and by what means had Matt Holby accrued the money in the first place? The word *revenge* sprang into his mind again. *Revenge*: that was the word the bearded man Hank was *alleged* to have used after the killings.

'That's your next move,' Snake said, 'but what about *our* next move?'

Jack gave him a level look. 'What do you figure your next move should be?' he asked.

Snake looked at Edward Joe and Edward Joe answered for both of them.

71

'With your permission, Sheriff, we'd like to ride up to River Fork with you. After all, Matt and his family were our kin.'

'That's good thinking,' Snake agreed.

'Except for one thing,' Jack said. 'I'm not riding up there for revenge. I'm riding up here for justice and to heave my friend John Schnell out of the deep shit he finds himself in. It might be even deeper than he knows.'

Bridget was still tut-tutting as she got them provisioned up for the trip. Other things being equal, they would be in River Fork early the morning after next. That would mean spending one night under antelope hide, which, in normal circumstances, Jack wouldn't have minded a bit. In his early years, he had spent many a night with his buddies camping out in the wilderness on fishing trips. It had made him think of the First Nations People and all their hunting skills. But sleeping in a tipi with two other hombres who might snore their heads off was quite another thing.

'You think the weather will hold, my friend?' he asked Doc Buchanan. The doctor had a reputation as a weather predicator. Folks thought that because he knew how to handle croup and broken bones, he was some kind of wizard.

Doc Buchanan looked up at the sky and did his best to look wise. 'The wind is changing and I see signs of rain, but it won't snow, that's for sure. I envy you and I wish I could come with you.'

'And I wish I could stay right here,' Jack said. 'Sleeping out in the open could give me a twinge of rheumatics in my right leg and sleeping in a tipi with these Holbys snoring like horses with bad colds could send me right off my head.'

'Put cotton wool in your ears,' the doctor advised, 'or a tuft of moss, but make sure there are no creepy crawlies in there first.'

Jack grinned; it wasn't the best advice his friend had given him.

Jack unlocked his drawer and took out the Navy Cap and Ball. He examined it closely and handed it to Snake. 'I'm handing this to you, Snake, because I believe your story and you're liable to need it in River Fork. I hope you know how to use an antique like this.'

Snake looked at the gun and sniffed it like a dog sniffing at a chosen tree. 'This is an old friend,' he said. 'Seen me through a heap of tight corners and it hasn't let me down yet. Only one trouble: it takes a long time to reload. If you don't bring down your man first time, he could be on you before you can reload.'

'Well,' Jack said, 'I'll lend you one of my official Winchesters. A Winchester is better at long range as you probably know.'

'Then let's hope everything happens at long range,' Snake said with a grin.

They set out soon after sunrise next morning in the hope that, with fair weather and on the fine horses they were riding, they might reach River Fork well before sunset. River Fork was quite a sizeable town, maybe three times the size of Silver Spur. You rode into River Fork and you knew you were somewhere. The sheriff of River Fork certainly had his hands full, especially at the end of the month or at round up time when the waddies drew their pay and hit town. John Schnell had two full time deputies and a number of part timers who helped out when necessary.

Jack was thinking about that as he rode along the trail. When I was a young guy, I wouldn't have given a trip like this a second thought. Now I think about everything in advance, Bridget is right. When I get back home, I must think about my future.

Though the horses did their best, they were some way out of River Fork as the sun started to sink down over the hills.

'We're nearly there,' Edward Joe said. 'I think we should ride on.'

'I don't think that's the best deal,' Snake advised. 'These horses need to rest up. So I guess we should pitch camp and make a fire. What do you think, Jack?'

Jack had to agree, despite his reservations about snoring and sleeping in a tipi with the two men. Maybe he could sleep in the open under the stars, if need be.

So they set up the tipi they had dragged all the way from Silver Spur and Jack and Snake set it up between them. Then Snake made a fire and started a cook up.

'What do I do?' Edward Joe asked helplessly.

'What you can do is keep out of the way until the chuck is ready or you can take the horses down to the creek where they can rest up and drink their fill. But don't forget to hobble them in case they mosey off some place. In which case it might take all day tomorrow to track them down.'

Edward Joe paused for a moment. 'Well, that will be fine, Sheriff, but how do you hobble a horse?'

Snake laughed and Jack took the horses down to the creek which was no more than a hundred feet from the camp. He handed Edward Joe a canteen. 'Fill this with fast flowing water from the creek but make sure it isn't stagnant and don't fall in the creek because my swimming skills are somewhat limited.'

Edward Joe chuckled and shook his head.

Snake proved himself to be an excellent wilderness survivor and Jack was glad he was on board. He even felt a little envious of the younger man.

After the meal they settled down to sleep. Snake had a good line in snoring. So Jack took his bedroll outside and stretched under the stars. In fact, the stars were as bright as the distant camp fires of the ancestors on the Happy Hunting Ground. Although Jack knew that was a First Nations legend, it gave him peace of mind and he drifted off in a matter of minutes.

He was in a deep sleep when he became aware of someone shaking him, none too gently.

'What?' Jack said, reaching for his gun which was under his saddle.

'Hush up!' Snake said. 'It's time to shake the sleep dust out of your eyes. Daylight is at hand and it's time to rise and shine.'

'What's got into you?' Jack grumbled. 'You suddenly fixed on becoming a poet or something?'

'That's a quote from somewhere or other,' Snake said. 'Glad you slept well. Breakfast is ready. So get up off your butt and come and get it.'

Jack was quickly on his feet, glad that he felt no more aches and pains than usual.

'Where's Edward Joe?' he asked as he knelt and stretched his hands to the fire.

Snake chuckled. 'He's out there talking to the horses. Likes to think he's being useful. I hear townsfolk often talk to their horses. Some say the horses talk back but I never heard more than a snort or a snicker before.'

'You're talking good horse sense,' Jack said.

Snake gave his usual croaky laugh.

They weren't too far from the trail that ran on towards River Fork. The reason River Fork was so popular was that it was at the confluence of two rivers and several minor creeks flowed into it. As they rode on, the sun rose behind them and they felt it warming their backs. But, despite his comparatively restful night, Jack had a sense of foreboding. He couldn't figure it out but it was as though someone was watching them behind every tree and on the top of every bluff.

Bridget would have said, 'Listen to your inner voice and take care, because even if you don't know where it comes from, it's there to warn you.' Bridget was part Irish and the Irish had a reputation for being fey, whatever that might mean. Suzanna would have agreed with her and so would her husband Mart, though he claimed to have an open mind on the subject of ghosts and all matters spooky!

With this creepy feeling in the back of his mind, Jack rode on but said nothing to his companions.

River Fork was bustling as usual and Jack soon led the way to Sheriff John Schnell's office, which was quite close to the edge of town.

John Schnell saw them coming and walked out to meet them. 'Howdy, Jack. I'm right glad you got here.'

'Came as soon as we could.'

Jack introduced his two companions.

'So you're both Holbys,' John Schnell said with a hint of suspicion.

'Come to find out who killed our kin,' Snake told him.

'Matt Holby was my pa,' Edward Joe confirmed, 'but I don't think I ever met him.'

'Well, you might have come to the right place in your search,' John Schnell said. He was a big man of German origin and he wore his badge of office with pride. 'The boy I've got locked up in the jail is getting a little jumpy. So it's a good thing you're here to take him off my hands. This is a rough town at the best of times and at the worst it could be like hell on earth, if you know what I mean.' He spoke with a heavy German accent and like many Germans, he wasn't strong on humour.

Jack said he knew exactly what he meant and would like to see the prisoner as soon as possible.

'That will be good,' John Schnell said with some relief. 'Come through to the cells.'

Edward Joe was already halfway to the door but Jack said, 'Wait here, Mr Holby. We don't want to spook the prisoner, do we? If he sees three of us, he'll probably think he's being led off to put his head in the hangman's noose.'

'That's damn right,' Snake agreed.

'Sit down and I'll ask my good lady to bring you coffee and cakes. We have very good cakes here.'

Sheriff John Schnell led the way to the cells, unlocked a door and stood aside. Jack stepped inside and saw a young man with fair hair and an apprehensive expression on his face. He was tall and rangy but didn't look much like the intrepid gunman Jack had expected.

'I'm Sheriff Jack Kincade from Silver Spur,' Jack informed the unlikely gunman, 'and I'm here to talk to you about the recent Holby murders.'

The young man was standing with his back to the cell wall and looked as though he would have liked to fade into it and disappear completely. 'I had no part in those murders,' he murmured apprehensively.

'You say that and I'm glad to hear it,' Jack replied without emotion, 'but I believe you were there when those good people were killed. So maybe you could tell me exactly what happened.'

For a moment the young man seemed as though his tongue had frozen to the roof of his mouth.

'OK,' Jack said. 'Why don't you sit down on that cot and spell out the whole sad story?'

The young man regarded Jack warily for a moment and then swallowed hard and sat down on his cot. John Schnell had carried a couple of chairs into the cell and he and Jack sat down facing the young man. Jack took out his notebook and prepared to jot down an account of what he said.

'Am I under suspicion?' the young man asked anxiously.

Jack looked him in the eye and the man blinked. 'Everyone's under suspicion at the moment, my friend. So why don't you just tell me the facts? First off, it might help if you gave me your name ... your real name and not some kind of alias.'

The young man took a deep breath. 'I came here for protection. Right now I'm in danger of being killed.'

'Sure.' Jack nodded. 'And I came here to find out the truth. So just spill the beans and answer my question. The truth might keep your head out of the noose.'

The young man looked at him and gave a quick nod. 'Name's Aubrey Appleton,' he said.

Jack wrote down the name. 'So tell me what happened that morning at the Holby spread,' he said.

Appleton looked away. 'It was horrible, Mr Kincade. I ain't never seen anything so bad before. Those two little kids. They didn't deserve that treatment. They were two innocent girls. They ran away screaming and they were still screaming when they were shot down.'

Jack jotted something in his notebook. 'By what kind of gun?' he asked.

'A Navy Colt,' Appleton said.

'What kind of gun do you carry, my friend?' Jack asked him.

'I don't have a Colt. I have a Remington,' Appleton said. 'I handed it in to the sheriff here when I came looking for refuge.'

Jack looked at Schnell and Schnell nodded his assent.

'So who had the Navy Colt?' Jack asked the young man.

Appleton hesitated for a moment.

'If you didn't fire those shots, someone else must have done,' Jack told him.

The young man nodded again. 'That would be Justin Milo,' he said quietly, as though he suspected the cell walls might have ears.

Jack took another note. '"*Dead men tell no tales*",' he quoted, '"*and that applies to boys and girls, too*".' He looked at Aubrey Appleton. '"*And revenge is sweet*". Do you remember hearing those words before?'

That threw the young man right back on his heels. 'How did you know that?" he asked in astonishment.

'I know it because Hank said it,' Jack replied.

Aubrey Appleton started blinking and gasping like he had just come face to face with Saint Peter or the Archangel Gabriel on Judgement Day.

'Tell me about Hank,' Jack asked him. 'I know he has a

big beard like Santa Claus and I know he shot Matt Holby with a scatter gun on the stoop of his cabin. And I know you saw a lone cow in the river and Hank asked you if you wanted it for dinner.'

Aubrey Appleton stared at him aghast. 'You must have been there!' he marvelled.

Jack shook his head. 'No, I wasn't there, my friend, but I know a guy who was. So come clean on the truth and Hank and the rest of the bunch, and all about the revenge that was so sweet that four people had to be murdered in cold blood.' For the first time Jack's voice rose a tone or two.

'I didn't do any of those things,' Aubrey Appleton protested.

'No, but you were there, weren't you, and that makes you an accessory to the murders, including the killing of those two innocent little girls. So, if you don't tell me the whole story you might find yourself swinging at the end of a rope along with the rest who committed those terrible crimes.' Although Jack looked calm his voice was suddenly full of menace.

Aubrey Appleton started trembling. 'I'm the innocent party here,' he insisted. 'I had no part in those shootings, I tell you.'

Jack was smiling but the smile had no warmth in it. 'I think you'll need to convince the judge about that,' he said.

Jack rose from his chair. 'OK, Mr Appleton, I'm going to let you think on that for a while.' He closed his notebook and went to the door of the cell. John Schnell followed him and locked the door, leaving Appleton to stare at him in astonishment.

Out in the main office, John Schnell grinned. 'You did a

good job there, Jack, I did not know you had such skills.'

'I didn't know, either,' Jack affirmed, 'but when the devil kicks you in the rump you suddenly realize you have to do something in case he tramples you to the ground.'

John Schnell frowned. He would never get to grips with Jack's wry sense of humour. 'But why did you let him off the hook like that?' he asked. 'Just when you were so close to getting to the truth?'

'That's because I've got an ace in the hole and he knows it. If we let him stew for an hour or two, the whole truth will come vomiting out. That boy is so shaking scared he's ready to shit his pants. If you're feeding him don't be too generous, keep it to bread and water, John. There's nothing like bread and water for wearing a man down.'

'What's happening in there?' Edward Joe Holby asked them.

'We're talking to a guy who was one of the bunch who killed your pa and his wife and your half-sisters. In the next hour he's going to spill the beans on the whole sorry business and lead us to the killers.'

Snake Holby said nothing but Jack saw by the look of concentration his face that he was taking in every last detail.

'Who can I trust here?' he asked himself.

CHAPTER SIX

Sheriff Schnell's good lady turned out to be almost as adept as Bridget when it came to culinary skills and she produced an excellent meal for Jack and the Holbys in the room behind the sheriff's office. She even made a presentable bread and water dish for Aubrey Appleton, the prisoner. She took everything her husband said literally ... or almost. In fact the bread and water dish was transmogrified into dripping toast with an egg which Aubrey Appleton pronounced as quite delicious!

'What happens next?' Snake Holby asked Jack while they were eating. Snake was clearly becoming as restless as a cat without a mouse or a dog without a bone to gnaw on.

'Well now,' Jack said, 'I have a few more questions to ask that weird gunman in there. So I suggest you boys take a stroll around town. I'm sure there's a lot to see out there, isn't that so, Mr Schnell?'

Sheriff Schnell agreed that, indeed, there was a lot to see around the town.

Edward Joe Holby looked pleased, though not unduly impressed. 'So, when do we get to talk to the prisoner ourselves?' he asked.

'I think you need to leave that to the law,' Jack told him. 'Just as soon as we're good and ready we'll tell you all we can. Why don't you just walk right out to the end of town and back again? But I suggest you don't tell anyone who you are or what your business is. Just mosey around and keep your ears and eyes to the ground. You might pick up some useful morsels of information out there.'

Snake nodded in agreement. The uncle and nephew weren't exactly bosom pals but at least they appeared to be a little more tolerant towards one another since they were both on the same mission and Snake had instructed Edward Joe in the use of his Smith and Wesson.

When they had wandered off, Jack and Sheriff Schnell returned to Aubrey Appleton's cell. The gangly youth was sitting on his bed with his legs stretched out looking a tad more relaxed.

When Jack entered the cell, the youth said, 'Listen, Sheriff, I've been thinking on what you said and I know I'm in deep trouble here. I don't want to hang for things I didn't do. And I don't want to get shot to death by Hank and the gang, either. So what do I do?'

'Well, you turned yourself in when you could have lit out for the border or some place,' Jack reminded him, 'and if you spell out the whole story, you might just save your skinny neck. I can't promise anything but honesty is always better than lying through your back teeth. So why don't we go a little further along this particular trail?'

The young man shook his head in confusion; he wasn't the brightest candle in the ballroom. 'What trail would that be, Sheriff?' he asked.

'That would be the trail of truth and honesty,' Jack

replied. 'Do you have any difficulty with that?'

'No, I want to be straight up with you, Sheriff. So where shall I begin?'

'Well, there are three big questions in my mind,' Jack said. 'First, how did you fall in with this bunch of killer scumbags? Second, who are they? And three, why would they want to kill the Holby family? And fourth, now I come to think about it, what do you hope to get out of this confession apart from your neck?'

'That's a hell of a lot of questions,' Aubrey Appleton said.

'Well, that ruthless killing was a hell of a big crime,' Jack replied. 'So take the questions one by one. How did you fall in with these scumbags in the first place?'

Appleton thought for a moment. 'That would be around two years back,' he said. 'I'm just a simple farm boy really. I worked on the farm with my old man, but he died. So I had to move on. I didn't rightly know where I was going, but I met a man on the trail and he said he knew a bunch of men who would show me how to lead a better life.' Appleton grimaced. 'Course, I thought it would be some kind of big farming job. But it turned out otherwise. Those guys were bank robbers and train robbers as I found out later.'

Jack wrote a note on his pad. 'So you became a big time bank robber?'

Appleton nodded. 'Yeah, I sort of fell in with them. But I wasn't big time. I was in on a few robberies but I never fired a shot at anybody, and that's the truth.'

Jack wrote another note.

'And this Hank hombre, was he the leader of the gang?'

Appleton shook his head. 'No, Hank wasn't the leader. He was just sort of in charge of a small bunch of us. The real leader was a man called Pardoe, but we didn't get to see much of him.'

Jack wrote down *Pardoe*. 'So there were more than three of you involved?'

'Oh, sure. There must have been twelve or thirteen men in the outfit or even more. I never got to see them all. They called themselves the Phantoms, though I don't know rightly why. It didn't make no sense to me.'

Jack looked at Sheriff Schnell and Schnell raised an eyebrow. They had both heard of the Phantoms. Everyone knew about the Phantoms, who were as notorious as the James brothers and the Daltons. Pardoe and the Phantoms were no small beer. Mothers sometimes used them as bogey-men to keep their kids in order. Jack realized he and Sheriff Schnell were on to something even bigger and more frightening than they thought.

'So you rode with the Phantoms?' Jack said.

Appleton nodded. 'They promised me everything, and it was good living at first what with the food and the banks. Hank gave me a gun and all.'

'What kind of gun?'

'A Remington like I said.'

Jack nodded again. 'So what happened after the killings?'

Appleton gasped. 'That was a terrible thing and I knew I had to get away before I got in deeper. But I knew those killers would try to kill me too if I tried to make a break for it. So I just rode off by night.'

'Like a phantom rider?' Jack said with a grin.

'Oh no. it wasn't like that at all,' Appleton protested. 'I just knew those killers would track me down and shoot me wherever they caught up with me. That's the sort of men they are. So that's why I came here. It was the safest place I could think of.'

Jack looked at Sheriff Schnell. Then he turned to Appleton again. 'This man with the Father Christmas beard called Hank, he spoke of revenge being sweet. Can you throw any light on that, Mr Appleton?'

Appleton looked puzzled. 'I don't know nothing about revenge, Sheriff. I thought Hank just wanted to scare the daylights out of Matt Holby. I didn't know he was planning to kill him and the whole family. That was a terrible wicked thing to do.'

'Well,' Jack said, 'I think we must agree with you on that. Those killers must be brought to justice. I hope we agree on that, too?'

Appleton nodded vigorously. 'The whole bunch should be smoked out like a whole nest of rattlesnakes.'

'In which case maybe you could tell me where they're holed up,' Jack said. He looked at Schnell, who nodded somewhat less certainly than Jack would have liked.

'I don't know I can do that,' the youth said.

'Is that because you don't know or because you're too scared to tell me?'

Aubrey pulled a long face. 'The truth is, Sheriff, I am scared but it ain't that so much. You see, the Phantoms sort of move around a lot from one place to another. That Jesse Pardoe is a right clever man. He knows how to organize things in a big way and he always has his guard up. And I think he's rich as hell, too.'

'You bet he is,' Jack muttered. 'So, Pardoe sent Hank out to kill the Holbys out of revenge?'

'I guess that's so.'

'And if we get a handle on this guy Hank, he might lead us to the boss. Would that be a fair estimate, would you say,

Mr Appleton?'

Aubrey Appleton looked worried. 'I guess that would be so, sir.'

'Then why don't you lead us to Hank with the Father Christmas beard?' Jack asked him.

'I'm not sure about that,' the young man said.

'Well, I'm sure about one thing… ' Jack gave a sardonic grin. 'And that's this: if you don't care to help us smoke those killers out, your neck is already halfway into the noose and the hangman is just about ready to whip up the horse. And that horse won't worry too much about whether you live or die. That's the way with horses, you know.' He looked at Aubrey Appleton with a macabre grin.

Aubrey Appleton went just about as pale as a spectre.

'OK,' Jack said. 'I'll let you think on that for a while. I don't want you to bring up the bread and water you just had.'

He and his friend John Schnell left the cell and Schnell locked the young man in again. Jack went to the entrance of the office and looked up and down Main Street and Sheriff Schnell quickly joined him.

'Are we getting anywhere with this?' Schnell asked him.

'I'm not sure we are,' Jack replied. 'There's something doesn't smell right here.'

Schnell agreed. 'This young hombre lacks something in the head,' he said. 'He has a loose tile somewhere in there.'

'Well,' Jack said, 'he has got some savvy or he'd be lying stiff and dead in a ditch some place.'

Jack looked to the right and saw between the carriages and the buckboards and the numerous mounted men and women, the two Holbys ambling towards them.

'Why don't you go inside and catch up with your paper

work?' he said to Schnell.

'What do you figure to do?' Schnell asked him.

'I figure to sit here on this bench and think for a while,' Jack said.

He had a feeling that his friend John Schnell was getting a little worried about the case and where it might be leading to. Probably thinks I'm getting a little out of my depth here, Jack thought to himself, and he might have a point at that.

He sat on the bench and watched as the two Holbys approached. The two men were now deep in conversation, though Jack noticed that Snake's eyes never stopped roving around like the snake he was named after, making sure he didn't miss anything. Edward Joe walked up to the bench and sat down beside Jack.

'Hi there, Sheriff. Did you learn anything useful from the prisoner?'

'Not much,' Jack acknowledged, 'but just enough to set me thinking.'

Snake was standing with his back to the office wall, looking back the way he and Edward Joe had come.

'Did you enjoy your stroll around town?' Jack asked him.

'I'm looking and I'm seeing,' Snake answered cryptically.

'Anything special?'

'I see a blind beggar walking towards me down Main Street seeking alms.'

Jack looked past him and saw the man with a white stick and wearing glasses that were so dark you probably wouldn't be able to see his eyes.

'So what?' Jack asked Snake.

'So, two things,' Snake said. 'First, I have a strong suspicion the guy has been following us from the edge of town. And, second, I don't think he's any more blind than that cat

I saw looking at me from a doorway along there.'

'I think you're getting a bit jumpy, Snake,' Edward Joe told him. 'This is the first time I've seen the guy.'

'That's because you don't know how to use your eyes,' Snake retorted. 'When you have to live by your wits and your gun, you learn to have eyes in the back of your head.'

Edward Joe gave a giggling laugh which made him sound sort of girlish. 'You're probably right on that,' he conceded.

Jack was watching the so-called blind man as he walked along the sidewalk tapping the edge with his white stick. 'You ever seen that blind man before?' he asked Schnell.

Sheriff Schnell's eyes narrowed. 'Can't say I have. But there are plenty of folks who come and go in this town.'

They watched the blind man as he came tapping on towards them. Nobody seemed to take much notice of him as he approached.

'Why don't I give him a dime?' Edward Joe said.

'Why would you do that?' Snake asked him suspiciously.

'Because I want to put him to the test, see if he's really blind,' Edward Joe said. He produced a coin from an inner pocket and walked towards the blind beggar. The beggar stopped as he approached and turned towards him. He was smiling but something in his smile worried Jack. Edward Joe put the coin into the beggar's hand.

'Can you tell me where I am?' the beggar asked.

'You're in the town of River Fork,' Edward Joe replied.

The man's smile broadened. 'You have a fine sense of humour, sir,' he said in a surprisingly deep tone. 'But maybe you can tell me where in this town I am?'

'Right now you're standing outside the sheriff's office,' Edward Joe replied with a laugh.

'Indeed, sir,' the man said, 'and would you be the

sheriff?'

Edward Joe laughed again. 'No, sir, I'm not the sheriff.'

'Then perhaps you'll be kind enough to lead me to him,' the man said.

Sheriff Schnell was on his feet. He walked across the sidewalk to the beggar. 'I'm Sheriff Schnell,' he said in his guttural German accent. 'Are you new in town? I don't think I've seen you before.'

The beggar's lips quivered slightly. 'I don't come into town very often. I rely on my folks to bring me in.'

'Who are your folks?' Schnell asked. 'Maybe I know them.'

The beggar shook his head. 'I'm sure you wouldn't know them, Sheriff. They live a good way off from here.' The man licked his lips expectantly. 'Do you have any room in your jail at the moment, Sheriff?'

'Why do you ask?' Schnell said, glancing at Jack.

Jack was standing close to his friend John Schnell. 'I'm afraid there's no room at the inn,' he said.

The blind man turned towards Jack. 'And who might you be, my good sir?' he asked.

'I'm a man who can smell a rat,' Jack replied. He reached up to the blind man's dark glasses and the so-called blind man flinched and drew back instinctively. 'You mind taking off those fine eyepieces of yours?'

The man moved further out of reach. 'So you'd attack a blind man?' he said with an angry inflection in his voice. Several people stopped in their tracks and stared accusingly at Jack.

'No, but I'd stop an impostor and ask him to take off his dark glasses and show himself up as a fraud,' Jack told him.

The man raised his white stick to fend Jack off and

moved further out of reach.

Edward Joe gave that tittering laugh of his but Snake Holby was frowning. 'That hombre was no more blind than my Aunt Sally,' he said.

'I didn't know we had an Aunt Sally,' Edward Joe said.

Snake grunted.

Jack was watching the so-called blind man who quickly disappeared behind the next block. He had moved with surprising alacrity for a blind man!

'What do you think?' Schnell asked Jack.

Jack rubbed the stubble on his chin and thought it was about time he put a razor to it. Like the Romans, he had always preferred to be clean-shaven than to have a beard or a moustache.

'Well,' he said to Schnell, 'I think that so-called blind man could see as well as I can and he came to suss out who you've got locked up in your cell.'

'Which means,' Sheriff Schnell speculated, 'that those Jesse Pardoe boys are looking for our prisoner Aubrey Appleton, so they can kill him before he spills ze beans on the Matt Holby killing.'

'Which has a good and a bad side,' Jack agreed. 'The bad side is they want to kill him off before we get to them. The good side is we've got the right man and he's telling the truth.'

'So what's the next move?' Schnell asked somewhat nervously.

'The next move is, we take the prisoner back to Silver Spur and leave you in peace. You might even open the prison door for inspection, so that Jesse Pardoe and his bunch know there's nobody to kill in there.'

Schnell was nodding with relief. After all, the Matt Holby killings hadn't been on his territory. 'So where will you take the prisoner?' he asked.

'Well, that's for me to know and for them to find out,' Jack replied in his own cryptic fashion.

'And when will you leave?' Schnell asked him.

'The best time will be after sunset,' Jack said. 'And we sure won't be parading him down Main Street. Nobody around here is eager to get shot at, so caution is the better part of valour, as somebody once said.'

Sheriff Schnell frowned. He hadn't much idea about valour, but he knew about caution, as well as any man.

After the sun had taken its bow and disappeared behind the trees to the west of town, Jack gathered his team together and told them how things were and how they would be. 'Snake, I want you to scout ahead of me on the trail towards Silver Spur. And Edward Joe, I want you to ride beside me with that Smith and Wesson handy.'

'Where will the prisoner be?' Edward Joe asked him.

'The prisoner will be riding a little ahead of me,' Jack told him, 'so I can keep him in view. And I think we should stop calling him the prisoner because from now on he's under my protection and I don't want any harm to come to him.' He gave Edward Joe a quizzical look. 'You understand what I'm saying, Mr Holby? Whatever you boys think on the subject, I don't want any trail law on this. This man, Aubrey Appleton, is going to lead us to that nest of rattlesnakes. So we have to keep him as safe as we can.'

Snake nodded. 'Where are we taking him?' he asked.

'I've thought on that,' Jack said, 'but right now I'm keeping it to myself. I'm just hoping we get there without too much trouble.'

Snake nodded again and his nephew giggled.

'This might not be an easy ride,' Jack said. 'And my guess is there could be a few bumps on the way. So I've asked my friend Sheriff Schnell to lend you two boys Winchesters that might be better than those pea shooters you've got, specially at long range.'

John Schnell handed over the two Winchesters and an ample supply of cartridges. Snake examined his Winchester closely and nodded his approval, and Edward Joe studied his with suppressed excitement. 'I've been longing to get my hands on one of these,' he said.

'Well, don't get trigger happy,' Jack advised him. 'We don't want anyone shot by accident, and, if we can avoid it, I don't want any shooting at all.'

'You don't need to worry none on that,' Snake told him.

When Sheriff Schnell unlocked the door of the cell, Aubrey Appleton stood up like a man waiting to be marched off to the death cell. 'What's happening?' he asked.

'What's happening is we're riding out of here without any fuss and bother,' Jack told him. 'It's about time we relieved Sheriff Schnell of the burden of your skinny carcass.'

'Where are we going?' Aubrey Appleton asked nervously.

'Somewhere safe, I hope,' Jack replied. 'We'll be leaving in five minutes. Your hands will be free and you'll be riding just ahead of me. And I should warn you about one thing. If you try to make a break for it, I shall shoot you down like a rabid dog. You understand what I'm saying to you?'

'I understand,' the young man said. 'Just as long as I'm safe from those killers.'

'And remember this,' Jack said. 'The only reason I'm

looking after you is we're going to bring those killers to justice. One way or the other, that's all that matters to me. If you survive long enough and do what I expect you to do, you might survive a tad longer. If not, your life doesn't amount to a heap of beans. You understand me?'

'Yes, sir,' the youth muttered.

Jack said goodbye to the lady of the house and thanked her for looking after them so well. 'Take care of John,' he said to her. 'He's a good man and he doesn't need all this trouble.'

'And you take care of yourself,' she said. 'I hope you can trust your compadres.'

'I hope so, too,' he said.

They went out through the back way and saddled up the horses.

Jack spoke to the two Holbys. 'You boys know what you have to do.'

Snake nodded and Edward Joe smiled. At last the seriousness of the situation was beginning to dawn on him.

'We ride along by the back of town and then hit the trail to Silver Spur. And if we all do like I said, we'll hope to get back to town well before sunup. And if necessary, we'll just set up a cold camp and wait for morning.'

'Sure,' Snake agreed. 'No fires, nothing to advertise our presence.'

Snake seemed confident and he rode ahead, not too fast so that Jack could keep him well in sight. Aubrey Appleton was just ahead of Jack and his mount was attached to Jack's by a length of lariat so that, if Appleton spurred his mount forward, he couldn't break away. Edward Joe was a little to the left of Jack. Now he had stopped giggling and become quiet and intent as though he had suddenly come to appreciate the odds against them.

Jack thought, what a strange bunch I'm riding with! Each of them has a motive for killing the Holby family and Aubrey Appleton might even swing for it. So, who can I trust? The answer sprang into his head immediately – Snake Holby!

Snake rode ahead like a true scout, peering to left and right as though keenly alert to the possibility of trouble.

Jack could hear the noise of the town fading behind them, and when they hit the trail towards Silver Spur, he began to breathe a little more easily. It was a fine night and soon the moon started peering out between the clouds like an ancient god looking down at the earth and wondering why there was so much uneasiness and trouble with humankind.

'You think we're going to make it, Mr Kincade?' Aubrey Appleton turned in the saddle to ask.

'Just keep going and don't talk,' Jack said quietly. 'That way we all stand a better chance. If anything happens, don't try to make a break because I've got you on the end of this rope and I won't think twice about shooting you out of the saddle.'

'You mean you'd shoot a man in the back?'

'Back or front, it doesn't make a whole lot of difference to me,' Jack told him. I'm beginning to work up a real disliking for this callow youth, he thought.

When they were clear of the town, they looped back and hit the trail to Silver Spur. Snake rode ahead with complete confidence like a man who knew the trail as well as he knew the palm of his right hand.

They had ridden for perhaps a mile when Snake stopped and held up his hand, and they all drew rein.

'What is it?' Edward Joe asked.

'Keep your voice down and listen,' Jack said.

They all listened intently.

'That's coyotes,' Aubrey Appleton said.

Snake turned his horse and brought it back to Jack. 'Listen up,' he announced quietly.

'What do you hear?' Jack asked him.

Snake dismounted and put his ear to the trail. 'Riders,' he said. 'They're ahead and they're coming this way.'

Jack strained his ears and listened. There was no doubt now. He could hear the pounding of hoofs and they were approaching quite fast.

Jack lost no time. 'Get off the trail!' he commanded. 'Get off the trail and follow me into the trees. Don't say anything. Just do as I tell you!'

CHAPTER SEVEN

Jack led the way into a stand of cottonwoods. He rode slowly, making as little noise as possible. When they were no more than 200 feet into the woods, he signalled for the others to stop and then dismounted. Edward Joe and Aubrey Appleton did the same. Snake was already out of the saddle, crouching with his Winchester pointed towards the trail like a questing hound watching out for the prey.

He didn't have long to wait.

Six riders were moving along the trail in the direction of River Fork. Two outriders were looking to left and right among the trees along the trail and the rest were riding straight towards River Fork. Suddenly the leader raised his arm and they drew rein.

Jack covered Aubrey Appleton with his Winchester and whispered, 'One peep out of you, Appleton, and you'll be meat for the buzzards.'

Aubrey Appleton nodded. 'You take me for a fool, Sheriff? Give me a gun and I'll shoot those bastards down myself!' Jack knew by his voice that he meant it, too. Aubrey Appleton had transmogrified from a whimpering cur into a young man of iron-willed determination.

'Just keep yourself still and quiet,' he told to him.

At that moment, the moon peeped out from behind a cloud and illuminated the trail. The leader of the bunch spoke up. 'Now, boys, you know we've got to get that fancy Sheriff Jack Kincade and shoot him down before he catches up with us. It's him or us.'

'Why that's Hank, the killer with the beard!' Aubrey Appleton whispered in Jack's ear.

Jack didn't need telling: he had already seen Hank the Killer's white beard gleaming in the light from the moon. 'Looks like a kind and cuddly old man, doesn't he?' he muttered to himself.

'He's just about as cuddly as a rattlesnake,' Aubrey Appleton replied. 'Let me kill him afore he does a lot more damage.'

'That won't help,' Jack whispered. 'Revenge might be sweet in your ears, but cunning and the law will be a whole lot sweeter when it pays off at the end of the day.'

Then Hank the Killer spoke again. 'Hey, Jake Boy! You give us the right information on these hombres, did you?'

'Sure, I did,' the man replied. 'That lawman said he was taking the prisoner away from River Fork and I guessed it must be towards Silver Spur.'

'That's the blind man,' Snake whispered. He had slithered back so that he was within easy earshot of Jack.

'That's him,' Jack agreed, 'and like we suspected, he's no more blind than I am deaf and dumb.'

'Well,' Hank the Killer said, 'it seems you got it wrong, Jake Boy.'

'I don't believe I did,' Jake Boy said. 'That Jack Kincade is craftier than a whole pack of coyotes. They're on the trail somewhere and that's a fact. Probably left the trail and rode off by a side route.'

'Through the timber,' Hank the Killer speculated. 'Might be anywhere between here and Silver Spur, and they've got that squealing rat Appleton with them.' He looked out towards the stand of cottonwoods where Jack and the others were concealed, and his eyes seemed to penetrate right through the branches. 'Could be right there in that stand of cottonwoods,' he said.

'Want me to go and take a look see?' the fake blind man offered.

'You can take a look see if you want to.' Hank the Killer laughed. 'If they're in there it would be like putting your head in the fires of hell. You know that?''

Jake Boy dismounted and studied the ground off the trail where Jack and the others had debouched to reach the stand of cottonwoods.

'Lookee here,' he said. 'I see fresh tracks.' He bent closer. 'I used to be a fine tracker in my time. They said I was as good as any Injun. In fact I'm half Injun on my ma's side.'

'And you're half crazy on your father's side,' Hank the Killer joked.

'That's as maybe, Hank,' the fake blind man said. 'But if you climb down from that old nag of yours, you'll see what I see.'

Hank the Killer gave a sceptical laugh. 'OK, cowboy, I'll see if I can see what I can see.' He dismounted and bent close to the ground. 'Well, I've got to give you this, Jake Boy, you sure do have good eyesight and a good sense of smell, too, cause I can smell horses. So you do have a point. Those must be flesh tracks.'

'What d'you figure we should do?' Jake Boy asked him.

'You're the boss.'

Hank the Killer straightened up and peered towards the trees again. Jake could see in the half-light that he was grinning reflectively. 'They're in there somewhere,' he said, 'but they could be some way off by now.' He was tugging at his beard as though hoping it might give him some kind of inspiration.

Edward Joe was close behind Jack. 'You want me to take a pop at him?' he whispered. 'I'm just longing to use this Winchester.'

'Sure you are,' Jack said quietly, 'but like I said this is about more than revenge. So hold yourself steady and listen. If anyone needs to open fire, it will be me.'

'That's right,' Snake agreed. 'And I can shoot straighter than you, son, so leave it to the big boys. OK?'

Hank the Killer was still looking towards the trees where Jack and the bunch were concealed. 'If they went in there, they couldn't have got very far,' he speculated. 'You think you could track them right in there in this light?' he asked Jake Boy.

'I guess I could try,' Jake Boy said.

'So what do we do, Hank?' came another voice.

'That's the guy Justin Milo who killed those two little kids,' Aubrey Appleton hissed. 'Give me a gun and I'll take him out.'

'Just keep quiet and be still,' Jack insisted.

'That's right,' Snake agreed. 'Keep yourself still and ready.'

'What do we do now?' the voice from the trail came again.

There was a momentary pause. The horses were now grazing on the edge of the trail, and those among the cottonwoods seemed content to munch away, too. Jack knew if they made a sound the killers would be on to them.

'If we go in there, we'll be like sitting ducks in a shooting gallery,' Hank said. 'Those hombres might be in there somewhere, just waiting for us to come within close range. And there's no way I want to be any buzzard's breakfast.'

It was a tough call for Jack, too. He could open fire right there, but would that be the best course of action? It was three against six, not counting Aubrey Appleton who was an uncertain quantity. The six were seasoned killers and only he and Snake were experienced with their shooters. So it had to be an uneven contest.

But things seldom go according to plan in the best of circumstances and this was far from the best of circumstances. Something always happens to break the tension, and something happened right now. A big dark bird suddenly took fright and flew up squawking from the cottonwoods, and one of the gang on the trail suddenly loosed a shoot at it. The shot went way above Jack's head but Edward Joe took it as a sign that the killers had seen them and he fired a shot back with his Winchester. The shot went wide but the six men on the trail scattered immediately and started firing back.

'That's what I thought,' Jake Boy shouted. He had pulled round his horse to cover him.

'Hold your fire!' Jack said. 'Let those scaramouches come to us.'

'That's the best plan,' Snake agreed. 'We keep good and still, those killing bastards won't know where we're at.'

The six men on the trail were now taking cover as best they could but, for the moment, an uneasy silence reigned. Then Hank the Killer spoke up again. 'You in there, Sheriff Kincade?'

'Don't say a word,' Snake advised.

'I could shoot him right down,' Edward Joe hissed. 'He killed my kin and I claim a tooth for a tooth.'

'You'll get a whole mouthful of teeth if you don't keep your trap shut,' Jack muttered. 'Just hold your peace and wait for that skunk to show his hand.'

Hank the Killer was crouching beside the trail, waiting and listening. Jack could still see his white beard gleaming. He could easily have used the beard as a target and shot the man through the head. But how would that help? He needed the killer trussed up like a Christmas turkey ready for market and he wanted to know why the Holbys had been slaughtered and where Jesse Pardoe, the boss, hung out. You don't kill a man by cutting off his arm, he reasoned, and the Phantom Riders had to be tracked down and brought to justice; it was a matter of pride and obligation.

'OK, Kincade,' Hank the Killer shouted from the trail. 'You want to play it cool. I want to play it cool, too. So maybe we should back off and go our own ways. How would that be?'

'That would be just fine,' Jack muttered to himself, 'except that it isn't going to be like that.'

Hank the Killer was speaking quietly to Jake Boy, who didn't look too pleased. Then Hank and the other gang members mounted up and rode away quickly in the direction of River Fork, leaving Jake Boy on his own.

'What d'you know?' Snake said to Jack.

'Not a lot,' Jack replied, 'but enough to guess. Those

102

Scaramouches won't be riding on to River Fork. They'll be waiting somewhere along the trail and then doubling back towards Silver Spur.'

'So what do we do?' Edward Joe asked.

'What we do is we carry on through the trees and ride towards Silver Spur by another route.'

'How do we do that?' Edward Joe asked.

'We do it by common savvy and the stars,' Jack told him.

'What about that pretend blind man on the trail?' Snake said. 'We could rope him in like a hog and learn what we need to know.'

'That's a good thought,' Jack said, 'but I think it's a little too late for that.'

The pretend blind man had already swung into his horse, and he was riding hell for leather after the rest of the gang.

'Give me a gun and I'll shoot him right out of the saddle,' Aubrey Appleton offered.

'I believe you could,' Jack said, 'but I want all those bastards alive. So we carry on towards Silver Spur.' Though he didn't mention it, Jack was beginning to worry about his wife Bridget and the children and his friends in Silver Spur. Those killers might not be as bright as midnight candles but they were bright enough to hold people hostage and bring terror to a small town.

Jack didn't know another route back to Silver Spur but he knew how to read the moon and the stars, and by good fortune the sky remained mostly clear. So they made their way slowly through the woods and back towards the town. Jack had another worry: those killers could make good headway and ride on to Silver Spur much more quickly than he could make his way through the woods. Maybe we should have shot it out with them on the trail after all. And maybe we could have brought Hank the Killer down and learned the truth about the Holby murders. Jack couldn't work out what to do. I'm just a second rate small town sheriff, he concluded.

Then Snake spoke again. 'You saved me from a lynching, Sheriff, and I owe you for that. So whatever you think of me, I'm with you all the way on this. We neither of us like bloodshed, but we can't avoid it sometimes. So you don't need to guard your back because I'll be guarding it for you.'

'Thanks, Snake,' Jack said. 'It's good to know that.'

When they rode into Silver Spur by a side route, the cocks were crowing but the streets were mostly empty and quiet. To Jack's surprise, Hank and the killers were nowhere in evidence.

'Either they're hiding up somewhere, or they've cooked up other plans,' Snake concluded.

Jack was worried. Those killers might be anywhere, even in Bridget's Diner. Jack dismounted and drew his Colt. But it wasn't necessary – Bridget was already up and she opened the door and rushed out to meet him.

'Thank the Lord you're safe!' she said, throwing her arms round his neck.

'We're all safe,' he told her.

They took their mounts to the stabling behind the diner so the beasts could drink and eat. But they kept them saddled in case they needed them in a hurry.

'What are we going to do with this Aubrey Appleton character?' Snake asked Jack.

'We're going to keep him safe from those killers,' Jack told him.

'How do we do that? Your jail is about as safe as a house of cards,' Snake said.

'I haven't quite worked that out yet,' Jack agreed. 'But I'm rolling a few ideas round in my head.'

'Come in and I'll cook up breakfast,' Bridget invited.

They went into the diner and sat down at a table. Aubrey Appleton sat at the end of the table and he seemed wary but satisfied. While they were tucking into their handsome breakfasts, there was a knock at the door. Jack took up his gun and went to the door in anticipation. 'Who's there?' he called.

'It's me,' a voice came back, 'your local sawbones, Mart Buchanan.'

Jack opened the door and Mart Buchanan and his wife Suzanna stepped inside.

'We've been worried as hell,' Suzanna said.

Doc Buchanan looked at Aubrey Appleton. 'Who's this?' he asked bluntly.

'He's the guy Sheriff Schnell was holding in the River Fork jail,' Snake told him.

'Looks like he needs a shot of blood,' Doc Buchanan said.

'He certainly needs a shot of something,' Edward Joe agreed.

'I brought him down here so those killers couldn't get their hands on him,' Jack explained.

'I didn't have no part in those killings,' Aubrey Appleton protested again.

Jack told the doctor and his wife Suzanna everything that had happened between the time they left Silver Spur and the time they returned.

'So now those killers want this Appleton guy back so they

can string him up or put a bullet through his heart,' Snake said.

'And I need to keep him safe for the judge,' Jack said.

'A somewhat tricky situation,' Doc Buchanan said. He and Suzanna conferred together for a moment, and then the doctor came up with a possible solution. 'Tell you what we'll do,' he said. 'I've got a lock up in the grounds behind my office. It's there for people with highly infectious diseases as you probably remember, Jack.'

'Well, this boy's got a highly infectious disease,' Jack said. 'It's called sudden death, but I don't want you or Suzanna to catch it because you're our best buddies.'

'Am I just a piece of meat to be traded around?' Aubrey Appleton objected.

'You could say that. I don't think you have much choice, boy,' Jack said somewhat unsympathetically. 'And right now I don't want to see you burned to a frazzle. So, if you're not keen on being fried, you'll do as I tell you. While you're in that lock up, all your needs will be attended to. So I would say in the circumstances you're in clover.'

After they had locked Aubrey Appleton in the lock up behind Doc Buchanan's office, they reassembled for what Jack called 'A Council of War'.

'What will you do now?' Doc Buchanan asked Jack.

Jack didn't know how to reply. He had two options: either he could stay put and wait on developments, or he could take the bull by the horns, though he had no idea which horns or which bull. So far the only thing he could be proud of was that all his party were alive and kicking. But he knew right at the centre of his being that he was determined to bring the Holbys' killers to account.

While he was thinking things over, fate took a hand. The boy came over from the telegraph office.

'Excuse me, Sheriff,' he lisped, 'the boss said will you come up to the office. There's a message come through for you from River Fork.'

Jack sprang to his feet. 'This could be it,' he said to Doc Buchanan.

'What exactly is it?' the doctor replied.

'The intervention of Providence,' Jack said.

'Whatever that might be,' Doc Buchanan said sceptically.

They walked over to the telegraph office and the telegraph officer said, 'This came in for you, Sheriff, not more than half an hour back and I thought you should see it immediately. It's from Sheriff Schnell of River Fork.' He handed Jack the message.

Hi, Jack! I just wanted you to know those hoodlums you were talking about last night rode in late last night as plain as brass. They were in the Five Star Saloon, drinking and boasting till the early hours of the morning. That man with the white beard got as drunk as Neptune. I don't know where they are now but they're probably sleeping it off somewhere in town. If you want to track down those killers, why don't you ride up again? We could work together on this. John Schnell.

'Well, that's my answer from Providence,' Jack said to Doc Buchanan. 'Those birds are falling right into my hand.' He drafted out a reply.

Good morning, John. I'll be right up as soon as maybe. Get together your deputies and we'll see what we can do. Here's hoping, Jack.

*

He walked over to Bridget's Diner again.

'Get ready to saddle up again!' he said to Snake. 'We're in business.' He handed Snake the message from River Fork.

'I'm coming, too!' Edward Joe insisted.

'Well, you can come,' Jack said, 'just as long as you don't get trigger happy. I don't want anyone shot in the foot and I aim to bring Father Christmas and his compadres back in one piece to face justice and swing. That's the best thing I can do for your pa and your half-sisters.'

'Well, that's what I want, too,' Edward Joe insisted. 'I didn't know my pa but he's in my bones and I hear him singing for their blood loud and clear.'

'Then we'd better make it a joyful song,' Jack said.

Bridget was not happy about the development. 'You're way out of your territory here, Jack,' she said. 'This isn't your business. John Schnell should be using his own men to bring those killers to justice.'

'I think we should call it a combined operation,' Jack told her. 'If we bring Father Christmas to justice and track down Jesse Pardoe and the so-called Phantoms, I might just hand in my badge and retire.'

'Is that a promise?' she asked.

'That's a speculation,' he said with a grin.

'The same old trail,' Edward Joe said as they started for River Fork a little later. There was no way they could reach River Fork before sundown. So they would need to make camp off the trail and ride in early next morning. Thanks to Bridget and Suzanna, they were amply supplied so they wouldn't starve. They also rode fresh horses, except for

Snake Holby who insisted on riding his fine piebald.

'That's a good strong horse,' he said. 'Never lets me down. Never argues the cuss out of me and always knows where I'm going. I don't know what I'd do without that horse.'

They rode along the familiar trail until the sun began to take its bow behind the trees. Then Jack decreed that they should get off the trail and find a good camping place for the night.

'Do we have another cold camp?' Snake asked Jack.

'I think we can take a chance and light a fire,' Jack said. 'If those desperate hombres are sleeping it off like John Schnell says, I don't think they're going to come looking for us.'

Snake agreed and Edward Joe didn't know enough to argue. So they pulled off the trail and set up camp. Jack and Snake built a fire and cooked up the meal while Edward Joe wandered off into the woods to 'explore the lie of the land', as he said.

'You think we can rely on that nephew of yours?' Jack asked Snake as they crouched by the fire.

Snake peered out through the trees. 'I wouldn't rely on him further than I could throw him,' he said, 'but I believe he wants to avenge those killings as much as I do. Trouble is, he might just want to shoot them down and like you, I want to learn the truth.'

'The truth about what?' Jack asked him.

'The truth about why those killers wanted to kill my innocent kinsfolk.'

'D'you have any theories on that?' Jack said.

Snake nodded. 'Sure I have theories, but I want certainty. Theories are no more than a two bit piece. I want the truth right out of the horse's mouth.'

'The horse being Hank the Killer,' Jack said.

'The horse being Hank the Killer and Jesse Pardoe.'

'So there are two horses?' Jack speculated.

'However many there are, I want to stick my Navy Colt in their mouths and force them to spell out the truth.'

'Sounds a mite painful,' Jack said.

They rose before the sun peeped between the trees, took a quick breakfast, smothered the fire, and rode on to River Fork. Although it was early, the town was already astir and there was something like panic in the air.

As they rode in, people came out from all directions to gaze at them in apprehension and horror.

'I think there's been a deal of trouble here,' Snake said. 'I can smell it on the breeze.'

'I believe you're right,' Edward Joe agreed.

They drew rein outside the sheriff's office but there was no sign of John Schnell. Instead they were confronted by the big man, Alonso, who had recently tried to lynch Snake in Silver Spur.

'Well, now, Sheriff, you showed up a little late,' the big man accused.

'Late for what?' Jack asked him.

'What happened is the sheriff got shot,' Alonso said.

'You mean he's been shot dead?' Jack asked him.

'No, he's not dead, but he's hurt real bad. They've laid him out in Doc Viny's place.'

As they were speaking, John Schnell's wife emerged from the sheriff's office, looking shaken and pale as a ghost. 'Thank God you're here, Jack!' she gasped.

'Is John alive?' he asked her.

'I'm going down to see him now,' she said.

Jack dismounted and walked down to Doc Viny's with her and she told him what had happened the evening before. It seemed that there had been a rumpus in the saloon and when Schnell had tried to intervene, all hell had broken loose and the sheriff had been shot.

Jack rang the bell and Doc Viny appeared. He was a lugubrious character who always looked on the worst side. 'Ah, Sheriff Kincade,' he said, shaking his head. 'I'm real glad you're here. This town's getting more lawless every day.'

'How's Sheriff Schnell?' Jack asked him.

'Shot in the chest,' the medic said. 'He's in a critical state right now.'

'Will he live?' Jack asked.

The doctor shook his head. 'Only time will tell. The bullet missed his vital organs but it's going to be a long haul.'

'Can I see him?' Jack asked.

The doc shook his head even more emphatically. 'Like I said, he's fighting for his life. The only one who can see him is his wife and she can't stay long.'

Jack walked down to the saloon. The saloon keeper was standing on the sidewalk with his white apron covering his ample paunch, surrounded by a group of fellow townsfolk

'Ah, Jack! You rode in from Silver Spur,' the saloon keeper sad.

'John Schnell sent me a wire,' Jack informed him. 'Tell me what happened here.'

The saloon keeper was only too pleased to tell the story. 'Those rabble rousers came in last night and got pissed to their eyeballs. Boasting about how they'd shot you up and chased you all the way back to Silver Spur. Then they rode off and I thought we'd seen the last of them. But they came back later and got into an argument and started shooting up the place. We called Sheriff Schnell and that's when he got shot. I hope he's going to live.'

'How many were there?' Jack asked.

The saloon keeper shook his head. 'I believe there were six or seven. The leader had a long white beard.'

'Hank the Killer. You seen him before?'

'Once or twice. Some say he belongs to the gang called the Phantoms.'

'And I believe they're right,' Jack said. 'And where are those all too solid phantoms right now?'

'Well, they won't be hanging around in town, that's for sure. After they shot the sheriff, they vamoosed, but they can't be far off, can they? Why don't you boys come inside?'

Jack and Snake and Edward Joe went into the saloon, and the saloon keeper offered them a drink and a plate of food.

'Thanks,' Jack said, 'but we don't have time to eat. We've got to get after those killers and bring them to justice before they do more harm. But I guess we'll be glad of a drink.' Both Snake and Edward Joe nodded in agreement.

'How can we trail them?' Edward Joe asked.

Three men entered the saloon and approached their table.

'I'm Digby Dancer,' one of them said. 'And this here is Lance Forman. We're Sheriff Schnell's deputies, and we want to help you track down on those gunmen.'

'I'd be glad of your help,' Jack said. 'I hope you're good with your guns.'

'Good enough,' Digby Dancer replied. He was wearing a gun belt, cross draw style.

Jack turned to the third man. 'And who might you be, sir?' he asked.

The man smiled. He had raven-black hair tied back in a braid. 'Name's Jason Crowfeather. I'm half Cheyenne on my mother's side.' Jack noticed he spoke with some pride.

'You want to track down those hombres?' Jack asked Crowfeather.

Digby Dancer spoke again. 'Jason's about the best tracker for miles around,' he said. 'And he has a hound with a nose that can smell a man a mile off.'

Jason Crowfeather's smile broadened. 'When do we start, Sheriff?' he asked.

'The best time would be right now,' Jack said.

For the first time in days his spirits began to lift. Maybe the gods were beginning to smile down on them at last.

CHAPTER EIGHT

Jack gathered together the posse which consisted of Snake and Edward Joe Holby, the two deputies, Digby Dancer and Lance Forman, and Jason Crowfeather with his dog appropriately named Wolf Dog. The dog had a strong suspicion of mankind in general but he was obviously devoted to his master.

'How will the hound track down on those killers?' Jack asked Crowfeather.

'He doesn't need much,' Crowfeather said. 'Give him a man's shirt and he'll track him down for miles. Wolf Dog's nose is like no other nose I've ever come across before.'

'Trouble is we don't have a shirt,' Jack said.

'It ain't only shirts,' the tracker replied. 'We find the trail and he'll lead you right to those evil men. You just need your shooters to kill them off.'

'We don't intend to kill them off. We just want to bring them in to face the court so they can hang legally,' Jack told him.

Crowfeather grinned.

'The first thing we need is to find out which way they rode

after they left the saloon,' Jack said.

'Surely that's a hopeless situation,' Edward Joe remarked sceptically. 'There must be a hundred ways they could have ridden out of town.'

'Except that we know which way they went,' Lance Forman said.

'How come?' Edward Joe asked.

'Because I saw them with my own eyes,' Lance Forman said. 'And Crowfeather here has a strong suspicion about where they might be heading.'

The gods seemed to be smiling down at them even more broadly.

'Well, let's get going,' Jack said.

They rode out of River Fork and on down the trial leading north. Crowfeather and the hound dog led the way. The dog was sniffing along the trail with dog-like authority.

'You think we're on a wild goose chase here, Sheriff?' Edward Joe asked Jack.

'Well, it's the only chase we've got,' Jack told him. The question in his mind was how far could he trust Crowfeather and Wolf Dog.

The two deputies were talking together quite happily. It seemed like they were riding out on a Sunday school picnic. Snake was still looking right and left as though he suspected there might be a gun waiting behind every tree.

'How come this guy Crowfeather knows so much about these hombres?' he asked Jack from the corner of his mouth.

'That's pretty well what I was wondering myself,' Jack said.

Now Crowfeather and the dog paused and Crowfeather held up his arm and turned in his saddle. 'This is where we leave the trail,' he declared. 'And we ride on without too much talking. We'll stop in half an hour and take our chow. Then we go on to where I think they might be holed up.'

'Holed up!' Edward Joe said quietly. 'Sounds like those killers are expecting us, doesn't it?'

'Well, if they are, you'd better keep your mouth shut and your gun ready,' Snake said with a wry grin.

Edward Joe gave his usual rather worrying giggle.

'That nephew of mine laughs like a girl,' Snake muttered to Jack.

Jack made no reply.

There was indeed a faint trail running between the trees, and from time to time, Wolf Dog paused to sniff and lift his leg.

'Seems to know the way,' Snake remarked.

They came to a clearing where Crowfeather raised his arm and indicated that they should take a break. So they all dismounted and tied their horses' reins to branches where they could graze. In the clearing there were the remains of a fire. Crowfeather got down on his haunches and poked about with a stick. There was no smoke, just dead ash.

'How long do you reckon?' Snake asked him.

'Could have been yesterday,' Crowfeather replied, 'or it could have been last week. They threw water on the fire before they left.' Now he started rooting around close to where the fire had been. The dog was busy sniffing around beside him. 'You see this log?' Crowfeather said. 'This is where one of those hombres perched for a while and he had an awful powerful stink.' He called the dog over and the dog seemed to savour the smell. He started sniffing around all over the camp site.

'Well, there's no accounting for taste,' Snake said. 'You think Wolf Dog has picked up something?'

'He sure seems to be enjoying himself,' Edward Joe said.

The two deputies laughed.

They broke out their supplies and started sharing around and drinking water out of their canteens, except for Snake who drank water laced with whiskey.

'How come you know this trail so well?' Edward Joe asked the tracker.

Crowfeather sniffed the air. 'Been out here since I was half a knee high to a grasshopper,' he said. 'I know more about the woods and prairies around here than anyone else I know. Seen more things, too, some things good and some things bad.'

'So you've seen this guy Hank?' Edward Joe asked him.

Crowfeather nodded gravely. 'Seen him once or twice but I keep out of his way. He might look sort of old and homely but he's about as wild as a wolf and you don't want to be within reach when he lashes out in case you take poison from his claws like Sheriff Schnell did.'

'And what about the place where these hombres are holed up?' Edward Joe asked.

Crowfeather cocked his head on one side. 'I don't know they're holed up there, but I think they might be. It's an old broken down shack where a homesteader tried to make out and failed. I know they used the place because I've seen them there more than once on my travels.'

After the meal they rode on in silence for a while. Occasionally Crowfeather dismounted and studied the signs.

'Yes, this is where they rode,' he announced confidently.

'These tracks are fresh and Wolf Dog agrees with me, too. From now on we keep silent. Those men have remarkably big ears. That shack is no more than a mile from here. When we get to where we see it, I will hand over to you, Sheriff and you can take charge.'

And so they rode on, keeping as quiet as they could.

Crowfeather didn't speak again. He didn't need to. Between the trees, a fire was burning and men were squatting and talking with no attempt to keep their voices down. Behind them was the half ruined cabin Crowfeather had spoken of. The scout turned to Jack and cupped his hand.

'It's over to you now, Sheriff, and I wish you the best of luck. You're sure gonna need it.' He half turned and then turned back. 'And if you get those killers, I want to claim part of the reward.' Then he jigged his horse round and drifted away silently between the trees and Wolf Dog followed, cocking his nose in triumph.

'What do we do now?' Edward Joe asked.

'We spread out and wait,' Jack said. 'You take cover behind a tree and don't open fire unless I give the order, you hear me?'

'We hear you good,' Digby Dancer replied.

Jack tethered his horse and moved closer behind a tree. He counted twelve men, among them Hank the Killer. Hank was doing most of the talking and the other men were listening and laughing and even cheering him on. Jack raised his Winchester and took a bead on the bearded man. If he squeezed the trigger now he could bring the man down with one shot, but instead he raised the Winchester and fired a single shot at the chimney piece of the ancient shack. And the shot had an instant effect. Rousting crows flew up from the roof of the shack and the men round the fire reached for their weapons and sprang for cover. There was no more laughing and shouting, just confusion and anger and alertness.

Then one of the gunmen fired a shot and several of the others opened fire wildly into the trees to no effect. Then there was momentary pause.

'OK, boys!' Jack shouted. 'Now you've had your fun so it's time to talk and I'm talking to Mr Hank there, the one with the Father Christmas beard. Can you hear me, Mr Hank with the beard?'

Hank the Killer held his gun up, searching for a target. 'Who's there?' he shouted. 'And what do you want, disturbing innocent men about their business?'

Jack said nothing for a moment. He just peered round the tree and waited.

'Why don't you speak up?' Hank the Killer shouted. Jack could tell by his voice that he was laughing. 'Are you waiting for me to come and root you out and hang up your guts for the coyotes?'

Then Jack decided to speak again. 'This is the law, Mr Hank, whoever you are, and I'm here to bring you to justice. My men have got you penned in on all sides and if you drop your guns and come out with your hands up, you might survive long enough to face the judge.'

Hank gave a low chuckle. 'That must be one hell of a big posse, Mr whoever you are, so why don't just show yourself and we can talk this through?'

Then a voice came from further off to the right and it was Snake Holby. 'I'm one of the posse you mentioned, Mr Hank, you two bit killer and skunk, and I'm here to say if you'd prefer to die, I'm up for that, too. I've got you in my sights right now and if I pull the trigger, you'll be as dead as last week's cold beef dinner. I hope you can hear me, skunk man?'

Jack hadn't heard Snake deliver such a long and vitriolic speech before. And it was clear to him that Snake was not a man to respect the rules; he had his own agenda and he would stick with it. And the speech had a surprising effect on Hank the Killer, too.

'Well,' he drawled with an edge of sarcasm in his voice, 'big talk from a big mouth. Why don't you just step across and we'll see who is the most stinking skunk?'

Then, despite Jack's order, Snake fired a shot and one of the men by the fire lurched back and fell with a scream.

'That's my answer to your request,' Snake shouted, 'and the next one's for you!'

But before he could lever his Winchester, the men at the fire were on their feet, running towards the shack. Jack guessed their horses were tethered behind the shack and his ruse hadn't worked. Hank the Killer might have looked as old as Methuselah but he knew how to move. He had fired a shot in the general direction of Snake and moved with the speed of light towards the shack.

'What a mess!' Jack swore to himself. 'What a damned fool mess!'

He got up and ran back towards the horses. 'Mount up!' he shouted. 'And keep together!'

'What the hell happened?' Edward Joe shouted from close by.

'Mount up and don't ask questions!' Jack said. He looked around and noted that they were all there, all five of them. Snake was already in the saddle close by.

'Why did you fire that shot?' Jack demanded.

'I fired it because I had to,' Snake retorted. 'I knew Hank the Killer wasn't going to be fooled by your talk about being hemmed in by the posse and I wanted to kill him. So I shot one of his buddies instead.'

Jack chewed hard on his lip. This was no time for talk; this was a time for action.

'What do we do now?' Edward Joe asked.

'We keep together and wait,' Jack said. 'Eiither they ride off hell for leather and break away, or they circle back and come at us. My guess from what I know of Hank the Killer is he'll want our blood. So if we disperse they'll cut us down one by one.'

Nobody argued with that and it was the best decision because they heard the killers coming through the trees towards them almost immediately. Hank the Killer was shouting a blood curdling war cry as he came galloping in.

'Where are you, you yellow bellied skunks?' he cried. 'I'll show you who stinks the most!'

Jack and his men held together in a bunch. 'Don't let them panic you and keep the horses on a tight rein. It's every man for himself, so shoot to kill.' He had never used those words before and it was like somebody else shouting through his mouth.

The killers came in at a gallop from all sides, firing as they rode. Jack fired at the closest rider and the man leaped from the saddle and keeled over into the brush. Then another rode in, roaring and firing as he came. A bullet whined close to Jack and caught one of the posse, who fell without a sound.

The horses started rearing and whinnying, impossible to control.

Jack levelled his Colt at Hank the Killer, who wheeled his horse away. Had he been hit? It was impossible to say.

Suddenly the killers pulled away and there was a lull as gun smoke drifted between the trees.

'My God, I've been hit bad,' a voice came from the ground. It was Digby Dancer, one of the deputies.

Jack got down from his horse and bent over him. 'Where are you hit?' he asked the deputy.

'I'm not sure,' the man cried. 'I can't feel a thing and I can't see nothing.' He coughed and blood came bubbling from between his lips. He opened his eyes and tried to speak and then fell back dead.

'He's gone,' Lance Forman, the other deputy, gasped.

'He's dead sure enough,' Snake agreed. 'That makes just the four of us.'

'What's our plan now?' Edward Joe asked.

'We keep ourselves steady,' Jack said. 'It's the only thing we can do. I'm not sure but I think I might have winged that man with the Father Christmas beard.'

'You think you might have killed him?' Snake asked him.

'Well, he managed to ride away, so I can't be sure. Wait here while I check.'

Jack mounted up and rode out towards the shack. He found the man Snake had shot lying on his back, staring sightlessly up at the sky. He couldn't have been more than twenty-five and he looked astonished. What a way to die, Jack thought. Then he rode back and found two more bodies, older men. One had a bullet in the head and the other had been caught high in the chest and he was still alive.

Jack dismounted and bent over him. 'I'm killed,' the man managed to gasp.

'Can I do anything for you?' Jack asked him.

'Look in my top pocket,' the man said. 'Let my family know I died. Thank you.'

Those were his last words. He choked up blood and died.

Jack rode back to where the other four were waiting. 'That's three of them,' he reported. 'And that Father Christmas hombre may have taken off.'

'What are we doing now?' Lance Forman asked in a shaken voice. Obviously the death of his friend had squeezed the courage right out of him.

'You boys can do what you like,' Snake growled. 'I'm going after those killers and I'm gonna get that bearded man who killed my kin, even if it means dying in the process.'

'Now steady on there,' Jack advised. 'Those killers will know we're on their track and they'll probably be waiting somewhere to bushwhack us. Caution is the better part of courage, Snake, specially if courage turns into foolhardiness and gets you killed. If we want to find out why your brother was killed and bring the killers to justice, you need to stay alive. Otherwise, this whole thing has been a waste of time. My time and your time.'

Snake took a couple of very deep breaths and tried to calm down. 'I want that man's scalp!' he declared.

'I want it, too,' his nephew declared, 'but I agree with Jack here. It's better to be cautious than to be dead.'

'Well,' Lance Forman put in, 'I think I must take my buddy back home. I can't leave him out here for the birds and beasts to devour.'

That left just the three of them, the two Holbys and Jack. Three against a whole bunch of desperadoes thirsting for blood. Plain common sense urged Jack to return to River

Fork and call it a day. He could even hear the voice of his wife Bridget advising him to use his brain before it was too late.

Then Fate lent a hand once more. They heard a rider coming towards them from the left, not galloping but riding steadily. Then came a voice.

'Hold your fire, boys,' it said. It was Jason Crowfeather. 'I'm coming in.'

Jack levered his Winchester. 'What's this about, Crowfeather?' he shouted.

'I come in peace,' Crowfeather replied. 'I want to parley with you.'

Snake growled like a bear. 'I don't trust a man who walks out on me in a crisis. He could be luring me into some kind of a trap.'

Jack was more optimistic. 'OK, Crowfeather. You come in real slow and no funny business if you care for your life.'

They held their breath and waited as the tracker rode towards them with Wolf Dog. He seemed quiet and peaceable enough.

'How come you're here?' Snake asked him suspiciously.

Crowfeather had now ridden right up to them and the dog was sniffing around the horses who seemed displeased. 'I been thinking about the situation,' Crowfeather said. 'I'm not a fighting man but I thought I'd done things wrong.'

'What d'you mean, wrong?' Jack asked him.

Crowfeather gave a slow nod. 'Riding off like that and leaving you to fend for yourselves. Then I saw what happened and I thought you men were real brave, so something called on me to come back.'

'Could have been conscience,' Snake said. 'So what did

that invisible preacher say to you?'

Crowfeather looked down at Digby Dancer's body. 'It's a real shame that good man had to die. So I thought I should lend a hand against those killers. And Wolf Dog agrees with me on that, too.'

Wolf Dog showed no sign of agreeing or disagreeing; he was too busy sniffing around.

'When you say help, what would that mean?' Jack asked him.

Crowfeather nodded slowly again. 'I'll tell you something,' he said. 'It ain't no use just following their tracks because you'll be gunned down and left dead on the trail like poor Digby here.'

'OK, what are you offering?' Jack asked him.

'Well, I know the way they're headed and I can lead you by another route.'

'You mean you can follow them without being seen?' Snake said.

'I can track down a bear or a coyote without being seen,' Crowfeather boasted. 'But you need to be as smart as a mountain lion if you're gonna bring those killers to book. Four against so many makes for difficulties here.'

'It might be only three,' Snake said.

They looked at Lance Forman and he gave a faint smile. 'Tell you what we'll do,' Forman said. 'We'll put my buddy's body in that cabin and ride on after those killers. I think I owe it to Digby and Sheriff Schnell to bring them in.'

Maybe the powers that be were gritting their teeth and grinning again. Jack had decided to trust Crowfeather and be guided by his superior bush savvy. Crowfeather was obviously no coward but he didn't relish fighting, either.

That made him a cautious tracker, which could be an advantage.

'So, how do you want to play this?' he asked Crowfeather.

Crowfeather nodded thoughtfully again. 'Why don't I scout ahead with my buddy Wolf Dog here? You men can rest up a little and then I'll ride back to tell you what those killers have in mind.'

Snake growled sceptically. 'So you're a mind reader as well as a back woodsman! By the time you've ridden back with your report those killers could be miles away.'

'That might be true,' Crowfeather agreed, 'but it don't make a heap of difference.'

'And why is that?' Snake asked.

'That's because they'll have to stop and eat. And there's another reason, too.'

'And what is that, my friend?' Snake asked with irony.

'That's because I smell blood. That bearded man you call Hank the Killer is hit. I don't know how bad but bad enough to slow him down.'

'How d'you know that?' Jack asked him.

'I know cause Wolf Dog and me have seen it,' Crowfeather said. 'I saw by the way he was riding after the battle, sort of lopsided and low down in the saddle. I seen that before, and quite soon the hombre either drops down from the saddle and maybe dies or he has to stop so they can bind up his wounds.'

'So, I must have hit him,' Jack said.

'Well, someone did,' Crowfeather agreed. 'I think I know where those hombres are headed, too. An old camping place I know.'

'Well, if we can sneak up on them we might kill the whole nest of rats,' Snake said.

'That's your call,' Crowfeather said. 'But four against twelve is a purty uneven score.'

'What's your opinion on that?' Snake asked Jack.

Jack wasn't sure what he thought. He knew Snake could shoot but what about Edward Joe and Lance Forman? Edward Joe was a city slicker and Forman might have cold feet. With odds of four to one and maybe twelve against a gun-hardened enemy, it could be like sticking your head and your body into the fires of hell and no man does that lightly.

After a moment he said, 'OK, Crowfeather, why don't you ride on and find out where they are and where they're headed. And, like you said, we'll rest up here. It'll give us time to think on the situation.'

Crowfeather rode on with his dog and the four men waited beside what was left of the fire in front of the deserted shack. While they were waiting, Snake produced a curly pipe that he packed with tobacco and lit up.

'Anyone care for a smoke?' he offered. 'How about you, nephew? Since you've inherited my brother's dollars, maybe it's time you grew up, boy.'

Edward Joe gave a high pitched giggle and accepted the pipe.

Jack was busy cleaning his guns. He didn't care to smoke. Lance Forman sat quietly by the remains of the fire, looking somewhat grim.

'You OK to come with us, Lance?' Jack asked him.

'Sure, I'm OK. I'm just thinking what I can say to Digby's wife when I get back to River Fork.'

Jack broke out the rations his wife had provided and they all clustered round the fire to eat their fill.

'Let me tell you something,' Snake said.

'Then speak up, my friend,' Jack replied. 'Specially if it's something I don't know already.'

'Well, if you've got half a brain it won't be news to you,' Snake said. 'Here we are, sitting like ducks in a shooting gallery. Those killers might be creeping up on us at any moment ready to take a pop at us. Have you thought about that?'

'I've been thinking about it all the time,' Edward Joe said with a grin.

'And I've been thinking about it, too,' Jack said. 'So that means we have one good brain between us.'

Edward Joe and Lance Forman laughed and Shake chuckled.

After no more than an hour, they heard a rustling and Wolf Dog came between the trees. He gave a yap and got down facing the fire, panting with his tongue hanging out. Then Crowfeather came gliding silent as a ghost through the trees.

Snake had his Cap and Ball in his hand, pointing it towards the oncoming rider.

'Would you mind not pointing that ancient gun at me?' Crowfeather said. 'It makes me kind of nervous.' He dismounted and squatted down by the fire.

'So, did you find them?' Edward Joe asked.

Crowfeather nodded. 'I sure did, and they were just where I guessed they would be. And I was right about that bearded hombre, too. He's been hit in the chest and he's bleeding real bad. I got close enough to hear them talking. One of them said, "I think you're hurt bad, Hank. You think you can go on?" And Hank said, "I'm not sure, brother.

Maybe you should go on and let me rest here for a while."
"Well, I don't know about that, Hank. Who knows, those hombres might be riding up on us right now."'

'Sounds like we got them rattled,' Snake said.

'I'm not sure about that,' Crowfeather said. 'But I heard them say if they couldn't get Hank to a sawbones, they should stay put until the morning, give him a chance to rest up and stop bleeding.'

'So, where does that leave us?' Edward Joe asked.

'That leaves us with the initiative,' Jack said. 'We know where they are, and they don't know where we are. That means we have an ace in the hole.'

'So how do we play that ace?' Snake asked him.

'We ride on and win the jackpot,' Jack said.

CHAPTER NINE

'Can you shoot straight?' Jack asked the tracker.

Crowfeather looked at him squarely. 'That's real insulting. You think I've lived out here in the wilderness without being able to hunt all these years. I can use a bow and a rifle as well as any man I know, you included.'

'Please accept my apologies,' Jack said. 'I just wanted to know whether you are with us in this business.'

'I'm with you all the way,' Crowfeather assured him. 'And Wolf Dog is with you, too. That dog is part wolf as his name tells you and he knows just about as much as any man I know about tracking down beasts and men in the wilderness. I talk to him like a buddy and he understands what I say. So you can rely on the two of us. And that applies to my hoss, too. He might not be much of a thinker but he works things out in his own way. You bet your life on that.'

'OK,' Snake said impatiently. 'When do we start?'

'We start right now before the sun goes down,' Jack told him. 'And remember this, we're here to bring those killers to justice. That's our aim.'

'One way or the other, those men will hang by the neck,' Snake said. 'A bullet in the brain could be a whole lot better than a rope round your neck. A damned sight quicker, too.'

So the four men and the dog set out immediately and Crowfeather led the way through the bush country to a bluff overlooking the place the gunmen were resting up.

Jack seemed to hear a voice in his head again. 'This is a damned fool errand you're on,' it said. 'You've got a stubborn streak in you, Jack Kincade. Four men and a dog against maybe a dozen. It just doesn't stack up!'

'Shoot to kill,' he heard Snake telling Edward Joe and Lance Forman.

Forman didn't reply. Maybe he was kind of flaky because of the death of his partner Digby Dancer. Edward Joe, on the other hand, gave a low giggle which wasn't altogether reassuring, either.

When they got to the bluff, Crowfeather waved them down.

'Now we ride to the top of this bluff and we can look down on their camp,' he said quietly. 'What happens next is your concern, Sheriff. I know what I would do, but from there on it's your show.'

They rode through a dense stand of cottonwoods halfway up the bluff.

'We should leave our horses here,' Crowfeather advised, 'and climb to the top where we can look down over their roosting place and they won't know we're there.'

'That sounds like a good idea,' Jack agreed, 'and remember we don't shoot until I give the word. Is that understood?'

'That's understood,' Snake growled without conviction.

They tethered their horses to the cottonwood branches and made their way to the top of the bluff, where Crowfeather got down on his hands and knees and wormed his way forward to the ridge. 'We don't want to show ourselves,' he said quietly. 'You show yourself, you might just as well shout, "I'm here, boys. Why don't you blow my head off?"'

They all got down on their hands and knees, and crawled to the ridge, pushing their Winchesters before them.

'Keep yourself out of sight,' Crowfeather instructed Wolf Dog, and Wolf Dog seemed to understand. He was down on his belly, surveying the scene below.

When Jack looked over the ridge, he got a surprise. Yes, the men were down there and he could make out the huddled form of Hank the Killer, lying on the ground. Jack got out his spyglass and looked more closely. He could see Hank the Killer gasping and trying to speak. I guess the man's dying, he thought. He passed the spyglass to Edward Joe. Snake had his own spyglass and he too was surveying the scene below.

'I count six,' he murmured. 'Where are the rest of the bunch?'

'My guess is they've ridden on to wherever they're headed,' Jack said. 'That means the odds are more even.'

'The odds are in our favour,' Snake said. 'I could pop off two of them at least before they know what hit them.'

'Just like clay pigeons in a shooting gallery,' Edward Joe agreed.

'Hold your fire,' Jack said. 'We don't kill men in cold blood. We leave that to the killers themselves.'

'So what are we gonna do?' Snake asked him.

'You give me cover while I talk to those hombres,' Jack said.

'That's a real crazy idea.'

'Well, I am middling crazy,' Jack agreed. 'Must be or I wouldn't have taken this job in the first place.' He wormed his way to a low shrub and got up on his knees. Then he called out to the men below. 'Hallo!' he shouted. 'This is Sheriff Jack Kincade and I'm calling you to lay down your arms and raise your hands! Do you hear me?'

The men below immediately sprang for cover except for Hank the Killer who was left lying on the ground. Then one of the bunch called out in a clear loud voice, 'We hear you, Kincade, and you're a two bit lawman who doesn't know his arse from his elbow.'

That caused a ripple of laughter from both below and above. Edward Joe seemed specially amused.

'I might not know my arse from my elbow,' Jack shouted back, 'but I do know you've got a badly wounded man down there and he's in need of a doctor or a priest. So why don't you just do as I say and we might save his life?'

'You couldn't save the life of a steer with one leg, Jack Kincade!' the man returned. 'You're just about as good as a heap of stinking horse apples. So shut your big mouth before we shut it for you!'

Jack stood up and showed himself. 'Well, this heap of stinking horse apples is coming down to get you!' he shouted. He walked forward to the edge of the bluff and looked down. There was, in fact, a faint animal track leading right down to where the gunmen were.

'What the hell!' Snake growled. 'The guy's off his head; he's gone completely loco.'

Edward Joe giggled nervously and Wolf Dog snarled. But, before anyone could make a move, a fusillade of shots rang out from below. Jack scarcely wavered. He started down the animal trail with his Winchester cradled in his arms.

'Is that man brave or just plain stupid?' Lance Forman asked.

'Well, whether he's brave or stupid I don't mean for him to die alone,' Snake said. He got up with one knee raised, and fired a shot at the men below. Then he started down the animal trail, following the sheriff.

The men below were now taking cover and raking the hillside with bullets.

'Hell's bells!' Crowfeather yelled. Then he started down the hillside, firing as he advanced.

'This isn't the way we planned,' Edward Joe said, 'but now I get to loose off a few rounds with this fine Winchester.' Despite his eagerness, he steadied his arm against a rock, raised his weapon, and opened fire without much result. The men below continued racking the hillside with their fire.

'You carry on down there, Sheriff, those killers are gonna win this fight,' Snake warned Jack.

But Jack just continued down the slope towards the gunmen.

'OK,' Snake said, 'we'll do it your way.' He steadied his Winchester and fired, and one of the men below reared up and fell back.

'By all the gods, I wish I could shoot like that!' Edward Joe said. He raised his Winchester and fired and, as he did so, he felt the recoil, only it wasn't the recoil, Next second he was on his back and the Winchester was on the ground beside him.

'Jehosophat!' he cried. 'Those killers have hit me!'

'Lie still!' Crowfeather said from close beside him. 'Let me look at the wound.' He bent down and another bullet whined past, so close it would have hit Crowfeather if he hadn't bent to examine Edward Joe's wound. Crowfeather shook his head and tutted. 'That was close,' he muttered.

'Couldn't have had my name on it. Let me see.' He leaned closer to Edward Joe and Edward Joe winced.

'Am I gonna die? I've never been shot before.'

'It could have been in the head,' Crowfeather told him, 'but then you'd have nothing to complain with cause you'd be good and dead.' He peered at the wound. 'If you lie still and leave the fighting to us, my opinion is you'll probably survive. In any case, with that wounded arm, you couldn't fire a gun, anyway.'

Edward Joe lay back and groaned. I've got to get through this, he thought as the pain from the wound coursed through his body.

Jack was now quite close to the killers, close enough to use his Peacemaker. And Snake was beside him. 'Are you some kind of medicine man?' Snake asked from the corner of his mouth.

'No, I'm just an ordinary man of the law trying to do his duty,' Jack replied. 'And I think those gunmen are getting somewhat rattled.'

It was either wishful thinking or a prophecy. The men below must have read his thoughts because, the next instant, one of them shouted, 'I'm quitting. The Devil doesn't pay me enough for this kind of business.'

'You're damned right,' another of the men said. 'I'm getting out of here real quick!'

Both men ran for their horses and mounted up.

'I'm gonna bring those skookums down,' Snake muttered.

'That's your call,' Jack said.

Snake raised his Winchester and took aim. He knew he could have shot both of the men, but something made him pause. 'OK, Sheriff,' he said. 'Maybe I should look at my nephew, see how bad he's hit.'

'You do that, Snake.' Jack continued down to the camp with his Peacemaker in his hand. One man lay dead and another was groaning with agony. Two had ridden away and another had disappeared among the trees. He went over to the groaning man – in fact, he was no more than a youth – and Jack kicked away his weapon. 'Keep yourself still and I'll have my deputy look at your wound. And I should warn you, if you do anything stupid, I'll shoot you right through your half rotten brain.'

'Deputy!' Snake said in surprise as he covered the man with his Cap and Ball.

'The badge comes later.' Jack laughed. He walked over to Hank the Killer. 'Are you feeling as bad as you deserve to feel?' he asked the man.

Hank the Killer rolled his eyes and groaned. 'I'm killed,' he managed to gasp. 'Why don't you put a bullet through my head and finish me off?'

Jack checked his weapon. 'Well, I'd like to oblige,' he told the man, 'but since you killed my friend Matt Holby and his wife and children, I don't think you deserve that privilege. So I hope you stay alive long enough to swing for that wickedness.'

'I don't think I can do that,' Hank the Killer said. 'I'll be long dead before you get me in front of the judge.' He tried to laugh. But it was too late. Blood gurgled out of his mouth, and he choked, raised his eyes to the sky and died.

'Well, whether you're in heaven or the fires of hell, I don't figure it's going to be too comfortable there,' Jack said to the corpse.

He walked over to the youth again and looked down at

him. 'Where are you hit, son?' he asked him.

'I'm hit in the leg,' the youth said. 'And it's real bad. Am I gonna lose this leg?'

'You don't need to worry about that leg,' Snake told him. 'You should be thinking more about the rope that's gonna be tightening round your neck in the near future.'

'Are you gonna lynch me?' the youth said.

'We don't lynch folk,' Jack said. 'We leave that to the judge and jury. What's your name, boy?'

The youth hesitated. 'Brown,' he stammered out.

'Brown what?' Snake demanded.

'Just Brown,' the youth said.

Jack brought the Peacemaker round to the youth's head. 'Like in little brown cow,' he said.

'Don't shoot,' the youth pleaded.

Jack thumbed back the hammer. 'Try again,' he said. 'My guess is your name is Justin Milo.'

The youth's eyes widened. 'How did you know that?' he gasped.

Jack prodded him with the barrel of his gun. 'And you're the half man half skunk who shot down those two innocent little Holby girls as they were running away for their lives. Is that the truth?'

'I didn't do that!' the youth protested.

'Well, I have witnesses to testify you did that shooting,' Jack declared.

'I'm Snake Holby, Matt Holby's brother,' Snake said, 'and if you don't tell the truth, I'm gonna shoot the daylights out of your little blue eyes right now!'

'It was Hank,' the youth pleaded. 'He made me do it.'

'Well, Hank just died, so I don't think he's going to testify to that,' Jack said.

'Tell the goddamned truth!' Snake roared in the youth's ear. The youth flinched away from him.

Jack gave Snake a warning look and then came back to the youth. 'I'm going to tell you something, Justin Milo,' he said to the youth. 'Now listen carefully to what I say.' He crouched down close to the youth. '"Revenge is sweet." That's what your friend Hank said after those killings.'

'How do you know?'

'Let's just say a good angel told me. And that angel told me what you said, too.'

'I didn't say anything,' the youth protested.

Jack nodded. 'That angel told me you said something to Hank about his scattergun and how he killed Matt Holby with it. And then you asked him why you had to shoot the woman and the girls with that Navy Cap and Ball he gave you, and he said, "Dead men tell no tales, and that applies to boys and girls." Do you remember that, Milo?'

The youth winced with pain. 'I don't remember a thing.'

'Let me help that bad memory of yours.' Jack tapped Milo's forehead with the barrel of his gun. 'Does that help, Milo?'

'I told him I didn't want to do it,' the youth screamed. 'And I didn't. It was a bad thing to do.'

'I believe you,' Jack said. 'The point is you did those shootings, didn't you?'

'I'll never forgive myself,' Milo sobbed.

'Well, you might like to tell that to the judge and jury, because, if you don't, I think you're going to swing high for those killings, Milo.'

'I didn't mean it!' The youth broke down in tears. 'Please can I rest now?' he pleaded.

'Not yet,' Snake intervened. 'That dead guy there with

the white beard said, "Revenge is sweet." What's that about, Milo?'

Milo grimaced. 'That's what those killings were about. Hank was just carrying out orders.'

'Who's orders?' Snake asked him.

'Orders from the boss.'

'Who's the boss?'

Milo looked about him desperately as though the trees had ears. 'That would be Jesse Pardoe,' he half whispered.

'Jesse Pardoe, the leader of the gang that calls itself the Phantoms or the Phantom Riders. Is that who you mean?'

The youth nodded. 'He gave the order.'

'Revenge is sweet,' Snake muttered. 'Why should Pardoe want revenge on my brother Matt?' he asked.

'I can't tell you!' the youth cried. 'I think I'm gonna pass out.' And he did pass out.

'OK,' Jack said. 'We wait till he comes round. And don't blow his brains out yet, Snake, because if you do, you're never going to find out how revenge applies here.' He went over to look at Edward Joe.

Crowfeather turned and said, 'He took one in the shoulder. If I can dig that slug out now, he's probably gonna be all right.'

'Can you do that?' Jack asked him.

'Can I do it?' Crowfeather gave him an accusing look. 'You think I could have survived out here without learning how to deal with bullet wounds? You got any hooch handy, Sheriff?'

'Can't say I carry it with me,' Jack said.

'Well then, I'll just have to do it straight.' Crowfeather produced a vicious looking Bowie knife. 'You ready for this, boy?' he asked Edward Joe.

'What are you going to do?'

'I've got to dig that slug out of your shoulder before it turns bad on you and kills you,' Crowfeather told him.

'Can you do that?' Edward Joe was studying the blade somewhat suspiciously.

'Oh, I can do it,' Crowfearher assured him. 'The slug didn't go in too deep. If you lie still, I'll have it out before you can cry to your maker, boy.' He turned to Jack. 'You think you can hold him down long enough for that, Sheriff?'

Jack knew he had no choice. 'You lie as still as you can,' he told Edward Joe, 'and we can save your life.' He pressed his knee down on Edward Joe's chest and held on to his good arm, and Crowfeather went about his surgical business. Edward Joe thrashed about and bucked like a wild bronco, but Crowfeather was adroit and, before Edward Joe fainted, he had dug that bullet out as neatly as a cherry stone picked out of a cherry, except that there was a good deal more blood. Crowfeather pressed a pad on the wound and told Jack to hold it steady. Edward Joe bucked a bit and then lay still. After a minute, he opened his eyes.

'What happened?' he asked.

'Not much,' Jack told him. 'Crowfeather just saved your life, that's all.'

Crowfeather moved over to Justin Milo who was beginning to stir. 'You want me to dig that slug out of his leg, Sheriff?' he asked Jack.

Jack nodded. 'Snake and me will hold him down.'

'Keep clear of his other foot, cause he'll kick out like a mule,' Crowfeather warned them.

'I could tap him on the head with my shooter,' Snake offered. 'That should put him out for a minute or two.'

'I don't think so,' Crowfeather advised. 'Unless you want

140

to put him out for good.'

Snake growled.

Justin Milo kicked out and roared like a terrified steer, and it took Crowfeather a little longer to extract the bullet. When it was over, Snake tapped him on the head with his gun. 'Now you're ready for the hangman, boy,' he said. 'And hanging is quite quick if the hangman gets it right.'

'What comes next?' Crowfeather asked.

Jack looked up at the darkening sky. 'I suggest we make camp and have us a bite to eat,' he said.

'I think we've earned it,' Crowfeather agreed.

'What happens if those skookums come back on us?' Snake asked.

'My opinion is we have to take a chance on that,' Crowfeather replied. He looked across at the body of Hank the Killer. 'When the head is off, the tail doesn't wag too long.'

They made a fire and between them, Crowfeather and Snake cooked up a meal. It wasn't much but it would last them until they got back to River Fork.

Edward Joe had his arm in a sling improvised by Crowfeather who had fashioned it out of a spare shirt. Though Edward Joe looked grey and somewhat drawn in about the gills, he said he was hungry and thirsty. Justin Milo, on the other hand, was still groaning and complaining about his wounded leg and whether he would be able to walk again.

'Don't fret about that leg of yours,' Snake warned him. 'We'll fix you up with a good stout stick so you can get to the gallows in good time, and I guess you don't need to worry too much about anything after that.' That put a stop to Milo's complaining. He just got on with his hard tack and spring water.

Jack was thinking about the next day. 'What do we do about the dead?' he asked Snake.

'Well, we could just dig a grave and tip them in,' Snake suggested.

'We have to respect those dead people,' Lance Forman said. 'I can't go back to town without Digby's body. That would be downright disrespectful.'

The others had to agree with that.

'What about these other stiffs?' Snake asked.

'Well,' Crowfeather said. 'We either bury them out here or we lay them across their saddles in the old way and take them in.'

Snake nodded. 'That's what we must do.' He turned to Justin Milo. 'Now you've had your evening chow, you can answer my question.'

'What question?' Milo asked apprehensively.

Snake raised his gun and pointed it at Milo. 'Don't play dumb with me, boy. We're talking about my kin here, and I want straight answers. So tell me about revenge. Revenge for what and why my brother and his family had to die.'

'That's right,' Edward Joe agreed. 'Why did you have to kill them?'

Milo grimaced. 'I don't know the whole story,' he said. 'I just know what I was told.'

'What were you told?' Snake insisted.

Milo shivered and almost broke into tears again.

'Forget about your miserable skin,' Snake said. 'Just tell me the truth like I said.'

Milo struggled to get himself together. 'Well, sir,' he said. 'You might not know this but your brother Matt Holby once

142

rode with the Phantoms …'

Snake nodded and grinned. 'So that's the story. Go on, boy, before I throw up all over you. You don't take revenge because someone once rode with you. There must be more to it than that.'

Milo nodded. 'I only know what Hank told me and he got his orders from Jesse Pardoe, the boss.'

'Why don't you get on with it?' Edward Joe hissed.

Milo looked round in dismay as though he heard the Angel of Doom approaching through the cottonwood trees.

'Well, sir,' he croaked, 'it seems your kin Matt Holby left the Phantoms with a whole bag of money in his saddlebag.'

'You mean he stole it?' Snake asked.

'That's what Mr Pardoe said.'

Snake and Edward Joe exchanged glances. Edward Joe looked astonished, but Snake just cocked an eyebrow. 'You mean he stole from the men who stole from the banks?'

Milo nodded again. 'I only know what Hank told me. The Phantoms have been looking for Matt Holby everywhere and when they located him, they just wanted to burn the place down and kill the family out of revenge. Jesse Pardoe is an awful revengeful man. You cross him, you might as well be dead.'

Jack looked at Milo and said. 'Speaking of revenge, you know where we might track down Jesse Pardoe?'

'I don't think I can tell you that, Sheriff. Jesse Pardoe moves about from place. He could be anywhere.'

'The phantom killed who kills at arm's length,' Jack said. 'Well, at least we know the answer to our question.'

Snake was still nodding his head and grinning. He looked at Edward Joe. 'That's what you inherited, my son … blood money!'

Edward Joe looked slightly disconcerted. 'You mean I've come all this way and nearly got myself killed for money my pa stole?'

'I'm afraid that's the truth,' Snake said. 'But at least you now know why that crime was committed.'

That didn't do much to reassure Edward Joe. He looked at Jack with sorrowful eyes. 'What can I do about that, Sheriff?'

Jack reflected for a moment. 'Well, you can't pay it back, that's for sure. That's unless you get Jesse Pardoe's slant on the matter, which I should say is somewhat unlikely since we don't know where he is.'

No one knew whether Edward Joe was remorseful about inheriting that money because he said no more.

CHAPTER TEN

Jack Kincade decided that they should sleep that night in their bedrolls under the stars. It might have sounded romantic but the nights tended to be chilly and there was always the possibility of a surprise attack from the so-called Phantom Riders.

'We don't need to worry too much about that,' Crowfeather assured him. 'If I tell Wolf Dog here to keep an eye out and his nose in the air, he'll give us plenty of warning. That dog has the best nose in the territory and he'll sniff out trouble from a mile away. So you boys can hunker down in peace.'

'What about coyotes and the ghosts of the dead men?' Lance Forman asked him.

'As for coyotes, Wolf Dog can sniff them out too and he'll set up a wail that will wake up the dead and send them rightly back to sleep again. So you don't need to worry about them either way.'

Despite his aching bones, Jack quickly succumbed to sleep and he didn't even hear the others snoring which was quite a bonus!

*

When the sun peeped between the cottonwood trees, most of the posse were still huddled up in their bedrolls. But Crowfeather was already stirring the fire into life to cook up breakfast and Wolf Dog was drooling in anticipation.

'Pity you don't eat grass like the horses,' Crowfeather told him, 'because all I've got is a little jerky. When we get back to River Fork I'll see what we can do to ease those pains in your gut.'

Wolf Dog yapped in appreciation. It wasn't a loud yap but it was enough to wake the sleepers, except for Justin Milo who kept his head down and played possum.

Jack went down to the creek to throw cold water on his face and make sure the horses were OK. He was tempted to plunge into the pure running water but he didn't have time; he wanted to get back to River Fork and put a wire through to Bridget, telling her he had survived.

Snake prodded Justin Milo with the toe of his boot. 'Get yourself up off your skinny butt and see to your business, boy!' he said. 'You got a little further to go before they hang you by the neck.'

Milo groaned. 'My leg hurts real bad,' he complained.

'Like I told you, you've nearly reached your journey's end, so stop complaining!' Snake went over to Edward Joe, who eased himself up and rubbed his eyes with his good hand.

'What am I going to do?' Edward Joe asked.

Snake looked down at him and sighed. 'Don't worry about a thing. Just concentrate on getting back to Silver Spur. D'you think you can climb into the saddle and ride?'

'I can if I have to.'

Snake nodded. 'You've got guts, boy, I'll give you that. It must run in the family.'

Edward Joe tried to stifle a laugh. 'Ouch! That hurt!' he said.

Jack came back from the creek and, despite the paucity of supplies, Crowfeather managed to serve up a surprisingly edible breakfast.

After they had eaten, they brought the horses up from the creek and hoisted the dead bodies over their backs.

'Whew, those guys are starting to stink real bad,' Snake observed.

He went over to Justin Milo. 'Now get yourself up and get your leg over your hoss,' he said.

'I don't think I can do that,' Milo groaned. 'My leg is hurting awful bad.'

'Well, either you get on that hoss or we leave you out here to die on your own.'

'You could give me a gun, so I could blow out my brains,' Milo said.

'I don't think I can do that, either,' Snake told him. 'We've got to get you back to Silver Spur so they can string you up.'

Milo groaned and complained as Snake and Crowfeather hoisted him into the saddle.

'And if you try to make a break for it, I'll bring you down before you can count to three,' Snake warned the youth. He went over to Edward Joe. 'Think you can get on your horse?' he asked him.

'Sure I can,' Edward Joe said.

They hoisted him into the saddle.

When they rode into River Fork, it caused quite a stir. Dead bodies hanging over the horses' backs; two wounded men, Sheriff Jack Kincade, and the half-Indian scout Jason

Crowfeather. Lance Forman was riding ahead, wondering how he could break the sad news of Digby Dancer's death. But he didn't need to because all the folks in River Fork recognized the deputy stretched across his horse, and a great wail of grief rose up among them. Digby Dancer's wife was in the crowd and she fainted from the shock.

Jack rode on to the funeral parlour where the bodies could be lifted down from their horses and carried in. The body of Digby Dancer was handled with due reverence since everyone knew him and respected him, but the others were treated somewhat less respectfully.

Jack then rode on to the town hospital to enquire after his friend Sheriff John Schnell. The hospital was small but adequate.

'How's the sheriff?' he asked an attendant.

'Sheriff Schnell is doing well,' the nurse said. 'The doctor says he has a good chance of surviving. His wife is with him at this moment. I'll tell her you're here.'

After no more than a moment or two, Mrs Schnell appeared. 'Ah, Jack, you're here. Why don't you go right in and see my husband? He's a lot better now and he'll be glad to see you.'

Jack went through to the ward and found Schnell sitting up with a huge dressing on his chest. 'Good to see you're still with us,' Jack said.

'I vos lucky,' Schnell told him. 'The bullet lodged in my chest and the doc dug it out. And how are things with you, my friend?'

Jack told him what had happened on the trail. 'You'll be glad to hear that Hank, the man who shot you, is now in the funeral parlour dead as he'll ever be, so he won't be bothering you any time soon. But ...' He paused for a second. 'I'm sorry to tell you your deputy Digby Dancer was killed in the shootout.'

'That is a tragedy,' Schnell said. 'Digby was a good man. He deserved a lot better than that. So vot is your next move, my friend?'

'I'm going down to the telegraph office right now to send Bridget a wire to tell her I've survived the shootout. That good woman worries a lot. Thinks I'm too old for this kind of law business. And I guess the kids'll be glad I'm still around, too.'

'Could be Bridget's right at that,' John Schnell agreed. 'Maybe it's time I took the hint and retired myself. What about the prisoner, the boy who killed those Holby girls?'

'Well, you've got enough to think about, John, so I aim to take him back to Silver Spur and lock him up in the cooler until the trial. The Holby spread is much closer to Silver Spur than to River Fork, so I guess it's my privilege to put him in jail. He can rest up in your calaboose tonight and I'll take him in to Silver Spur in the morning. But I don't fancy his chances. That boy is going to swing, anyway, and you might say he deserves it.'

'That boy got in with the wrong bunch,' John Schnell conceded.

'That's no excuse,' Jack said. 'If the hangman doesn't get him, Snake Holby will.'

He went up to the telegraph office and sent the good news through to Bridget. He didn't bother with the gory details; that could wait until he got to Silver Spur.

'What do we do now?' Snake Holby asked him.

'Well, I'd like to ride home pronto,' Jack told him, 'but I think I should ask the doctor to take a look at Justin Milo's leg, so it doesn't fester and fall off before we get him to

Silver Spur. And your nephew should maybe join my friend John Schnell in the town hospital, so the doctor can make sure that wound in the shoulder isn't going to turn bad.'

'I think our friend Jason Crowfeather did a good job on that,' Snake said. 'He's almost good enough to qualify as a sawbones himself. He asked me to give you a message. Edward Joe is in the hotel right now. Crowfeather's with him and they're both drinking hooch whiskey. They want us to join them.'

'I don't know about the hooch whiskey, but I could sure throw back a pint or two of good strong beer,' Jack said. 'But first I must make sure that boy Milo is safely locked up in the town jail.'

'What a waste of space!' Snake said with disgust.

When Jack joined Snake and his nephew and Crowfeather in the hotel, Edward Joe passed him a glass of the best beer in the house. 'I've made the arrangements,' Edward Joe said.

'What arrangements would they be?' Jack asked him.

'We're going to stay here the night,' Edward Joe told him. 'The horses are munching away and enjoying themselves in the livery stable and they deserve a good night's rest. So you and me and my uncle here are going to sleep easy in the best feather beds in town.'

Snake nodded. 'On the strength of the blood money,' he said.

Jack didn't complain. It would be good to rest up for one night. He might even sink down into a hot steaming bath to ease his aching bones. It wouldn't make him any younger but it might make him feel more like a living human being.

Jack and the two Holbys were given the best rooms in the

house, and, after they had wallowed in deep hot baths for a while, they dried themselves down and went into the dining room to feast and relax. Snake and Edward Joe accepted cigars on the house and sat at the table, puffing away like kings or, as Edward Joe preferred to say, 'like saints riding on the clouds of heaven'. The doctor had dressed his wound and Edward Joe seemed to be doing well, though he needed some assistance with his feeding and smoking.

'You think they have clouds up there in heaven?' Snake asked him.

'I reckon they do,' Edward Joe informed him. 'They float around like cotton wool but they're strong enough to support as many as a million souls at once up there.'

'Could be a little overcrowded. Sounds more like hell than heaven to me,' Snake said with a chuckle.

After the meal they went to their rooms to sleep like kings. Jack lay down and the events of the day cascaded through his mind in a great avalanche of images, all tumbling together and whirling round and round. When am I going to sleep, he asked himself. Then he opened his eyes to see the light of morning streaming between the velvet curtains. He sat bolt upright and stared into the corners of the room. What in hell's name am I doing here, he wondered. He got up and washed and dressed. Then he went down to the dining room for breakfast, and Snake and Edward Joe joined him. As they were eating their ham and eggs, there was a disturbance at the door and they looked round to see Lance Forman as pale as a ghost and he stood there panting and gasping like a fish that has just been pulled out of the water on a fishing line.

'Hi there, Lance!' Edward Joe greeted. 'Why don't you come in and join us? The coffee's real good.' Then he stopped and stared. 'Why, what's wrong?'

Jack was already on his feet. He went over to Lance Forman and steadied him. The man looked fit to collapse. 'What's happened?' he asked.

Lance Forman's lip trembled. 'Something terrible!' he gasped. 'That boy Justin Milo has lynched himself!'

'You mean he's dead?' Edward Joe asked him.

Lance Forman nodded. 'I found him this morning, hanging from a beam in his cell!'

'Well, I'll be damned!' Snake said. 'So he's dead?'

Lance Forman was so shocked he could hardly speak. 'Hanging by his belt and shirt from a beam. We cut him down but he must have been dead for at least an hour.'

The three men left their breakfasts. Their appetites had vanished completely.

'We'd better take a looksee!' Snake said.

They walked down to the sheriff's office and found the body of Justin Milo laid out on a bed in the cell. His head was twisted round at an angle and his tongue was black and protruding. One of the nurses from the hospital was looking down at the body. There was no need to ask if the man was dead. It was beyond denial.

'Why don't you cover his face?' Edward Joe said. 'That look is horrible!' He retched and left the cell with his hand to his mouth.

'What do we do now?' Snake asked Jack.

'We ride back to Silver Spur just as soon as we can,' Jack said. He wanted to leave River Fork as soon as he could.

He went to see the doctor at the hospital and then into the ward to see John Schnell. Schnell was already on his feet and his wife was helping him into his clothes.

'This is a bad business, my friend,' he said. 'I've had some difficult cases but none as bad as this. Like I said, that boy got in with the wrong bunch and now he's paid vith his life.'

'You sure struck the truth there,' Snake said. 'Only one more thing to be said. He saved the judge and jury a hell of a lot of trouble.'

Nobody responded to that; it seemed indecent somehow.

The doctor put a hand on Jack's arm to reassure him. 'You don't need to worry yourself about this, Sheriff. I'll see to all the necessary arrangements. Give my regards to Mart Buchanan and Bridget.'

Jack Kincade and the two Holbys rode back to Silver Spur, leaving what Jack thought of as a trail of wreckage behind them. From time to time, the two Holbys exchanged thoughts about one thing and another, mainly the Justin Milo hanging.

'We couldn't have done a thing to save that boy,' Snake assured his nephew. 'Things worked out badly for him. It's what some people call Fate.'

'I don't believe in Fate,' Edward Joe said. 'I believe in destiny.'

'I'm afraid my brain isn't big enough to hold that thought. So tell me, what's the difference between Fate and destiny? Aren't they the same thing, like two sides of the same coin?'

Edward Joe contorted his face and tried to think. 'I guess Fate is like God handing things down on a plate, whereas destiny is something you have a tendency towards that gives you a choice.'

Snake gave him a sceptical grin. 'You keep thinking like

that, you might turn into a real scholar,' he said.

Jack contributed nothing to the discussion. He just wanted to get back to Silver Spur and see Bridget and Doctor Martin Buchanan. He needed Bridget's warmth and his friend's wisdom to console him.

They rode into Silver Spur some hours later and the sun was already sinking in the west.

'What are you two boys going to do?' Jack asked his companions.

Edward Joe responded immediately. 'I'm going to the Long Branch Saloon,' he said, 'And I hope my uncle will join me because I have a few proposals to lay before him.'

'Well, don't pay heed to Tiny Broadhurst,' Jack advised. 'Remember, that hulk won the war and tried to lynch you.'

'Well, he won't give me no sass,' Snake said, 'or I might bounce him right down Main Street like a big fat ball full of gas.'

Before Jack could dismount, Bridget ran out from Bridget's Diner to greet him. She was weeping with relief. 'Oh, Jack, you're back home!' she cried.

Jack sprang down from the saddle and clasped her in his arms. It was almost as good as the first time they had kissed. They stood right in the middle of Main Street, oblivious to the world. In fact, people had come out from every building to watch and enjoy their reunion. Some folks said later it was better than a play! When at last they parted, everyone cheered. Jack and Bridget's two children Stephanie and Gregory clung to their parents and didn't know whether to laugh or cry.

Doc Buchanan and his wife Suzanna pushed through the crowd to congratulate them.

'So you got back in one piece,' Mart Buchanan laughed. 'You're a lucky son of a gun. I should check your heart some time and see if I can find your secret.'

Then Suzanna gave him a hug. 'You must have been through hell!' she exclaimed.

'I've been through hell and back,' Jack agreed. 'But it could have been worse. I might have stayed in hell, but the devil decided the best room wasn't quite ready so he told me to come back to Silver Spur and wait until he sent a minor devil for me.'

'That's really obliging of him,' the doctor said.

The people round them laughed and applauded. And Jack experienced an absurd sense of well-being.

They went into Bridget's Diner and a girl brought them drinks. Jack sat behind the table and told them everything that had happened since he left for River Fork, which seemed like a century ago.

'So that boy killed himself?' Doc Buchanan said.

Jack nodded. 'I could have prevented that,' he replied ruefully.

'And what will happen to the boy you've got in the lock up?' Suzanna asked him.

Jack shrugged. 'He'll come up for trial and it's up to the judge and jury,' he replied.

The two Holbys had been talking in the Long Branch Saloon. The owner Kev Stanley was delighted to have the privilege of accommodating them, and his wife was cooking up a special meal to welcome them. Tiny Broadhurst had seen them come in but he didn't stay to welcome them; he slid away surprisingly quickly for such a big man!

Snake and Edward Joe were sitting in a corner far away

from the door and the other occupants were pretending not to look at them with too much interest.

'I think we have to talk,' Edward Joe said to his uncle.

'Is that so?' Snake grinned.

Edward Joe nodded. 'I've been thinking on things, Snake.'

Snake was still grinning. 'Well, that's good to hear, boy. It's good to know you've got the necessary equipment for that.'

Edward Joe seemed tongue-tied. He didn't know quite how to go on. 'It's about all that money I inherited from my pa, what you call the blood money.'

Snake raised his glass and took a long draught and waited.

Edward Joe swallowed hard. 'You were right about that, Snake. It was blood money since my pa Matt stole it from the Jesse Pardoe bunch.'

Snake held his glass up and stared at it as though looking for inspiration. 'And they stole it from the banks and that's why my brother Matt and his family were killed,' he said.

'And that's why we're sitting here drinking together,' Edward Joe suggested.

'Could be worse.' Snake took another long draught of his beer. 'You managed to get through with one arm in a sling,' he said. He looked his nephew in the eye. 'Why don't you come out with it honest and clean, my boy?'

Edward Joe nodded. 'Well, it's like this, Snake. I can't give those dollars back to Jesse Pardoe and I can't return them to the folks he robbed. So I guess I have to use them in the best way I can.'

'Like a good Samaritan,' Snake said mockingly.

Edward Joe chose to ignore that remark. 'So, what I aim

to do is build up the Holby Homestead and make it into a really profitable business.'

Snake gave him a straight look. 'That sounds like real good horse sense to me,' he said.

Edward Joe leaned forward. 'And that's where you come in, Snake.'

Snake shook his head. 'Just how do I fit in here?' he asked.

'I'm offering you the chance to come in with me, Snake. An equal partnership. We could build the place up together.'

Snake raised an eyebrow. 'That would mean settling down.' He looked quite surprised by the notion.

'Yes, that would mean settling down,' Edward Joe agreed. 'You've had a good run, Snake, but you're getting a little long in the tooth, so sooner or later a man has to settle down.'

Now it was time for Snake to nod and think. 'Well, boy, you've given me a lot to digest and I think I must chew on it for a while.'

'You do that, Uncle,' Edward Joe said.

The trial of Aubrey Appleton was held in the capital city. The elderly judge, sitting like a wise owl, listened to the evidence. Jack Kincade testified how Aubrey Appleton had admitted to being part of Jesse Pardoe's gang of armed robbers but had broken away after witnessing the Holby murders. Then young Hubert Parry took the stand. As Jack had noticed earlier, he was a bright young man with intelligent eyes and he looked round the courtroom without batting an eyelid. The judge asked him to tell the court what he had heard that day down by the creek, and the boy told the story without elaboration. The judge adjusted his owl-like glasses.

'Did you hear that man Hank say, "Revenge is sweet"?'

'I did, sir.'

The judge took a note. 'And will you repeat what he said after that?'

'Yes, sir. He said, "Dead men tell no tales and that applies to women and girls, too".'

'Are you absolutely sure he used those words?' the judge asked.

'Yes, sir.' The boy nodded. 'I thought it was a terrible thing to say.'

The judge took a note. 'Very well, you can step down,' he said, 'And you've done well, my boy.'

For the first time Hubert Parry smiled and nodded towards his father.

Then the judge turned a shrewd eye towards Aubrey Appleton, who stood with his hands gripping the dock rail so hard that Jack could see his white knuckles.

'So you admit you were there?' the judge said.

Aubrey Appleton nodded quickly. 'Yes, sir, I was there, but it was all too horrible. So that's why I split from the gang. And I can still see those poor little girls running away just before they were shot down.'

'Are you sure you didn't shoot them yourself?' the judge barked out.

Aubrey Appleton's lip quivered. 'I've never shot anyone in my life!' he said.

The judge then gave his ruling. 'We have heard reliable witnesses,' he said, 'and though the defendant was undoubtedly one of the Jesse Pardoe gang, he broke away and put himself into the hands of the law, which took some courage,

I rule that there is no case to answer. So the defendant may step down and go on his way.'

At that point Aubrey Appleton fell forward in a dead faint and the ushers carried him senseless from the court.

That wasn't quite the end of the story. If Aubrey Appleton had feared for his life, he might have relaxed in his bed because no more than a month later, news came through that Jesse Pardoe himself had been killed by one of his own mob in response to a poster offering a substantial reward for him dead or alive. They laid his corpse out on a long white table for everyone to see. And he looked almost peaceful and even pious with his hands folded on his chest.

'Can this really be Jesse Pardoe?' folk asked when they saw his picture in the county newspaper. Nobody knew whether his killer had received the reward, or where he had gone to subsequently, and nobody found out what had happened to Aubrey Appleton after the trial, either. He just got on his horse and rode out of the town and disappeared towards the west.

Edward Joe was as good as his word. When he visited his father's farm, he just sat on his horse looking over the spread. 'Looks like a broken down mess right now,' he said to Snake.

'Nothing we can't fix between us,' Snake said. 'We owe it to Matt and Mary and those little nieces of mine. I guess that is our destiny.' He turned his head and grinned at Edward Joe.

'So, you've decided to do the sensible thing,' Bridget Kincade said to her husband.

Jack nodded. 'They're putting me forward as Mayor. I'll take office just as soon as they find someone to pick up the sheriff's badge.'

'That shouldn't be too long,' she said.

Jack smiled. 'I guess you're right. There should be any number of candidates for sheriff in a peaceable town like Silver Spur.'